"Ah, Mr. Drakis—how good to see you again. What can we do for you this evening?"

The familiar greeting of the concierge was reassuring.

On the point of making his inquiry, Nikos saw the man taking something out of a drawer in his desk, holding it out to him.

"We were about to forward this on to you, sir," the concierge said.

Nikos frowned, glancing at the envelope. He took it, noting the thin, cheap paper and the handwritten address—his name, care of the hotel. It had a UK stamp on it, but the postmark was blurred. His frown deepened, and automatically he turned away, ripping open the envelope, impatient to dispose of whatever it held so that he could put his inquiry to the concierge.

But as his eyes scanned the handwritten contents, that inquiry became totally and absolutely unnecessary...

As did all his plans for Alys, who had beguiled him that single night all those weeks ago.

And who now had just exploded a bomb in his life.

Julia James lives in England and adores the peaceful verdant countryside and the wild shores of Cornwall. She also loves the Mediterranean—so rich in myth and history, with its sunbaked landscapes and olive groves, ancient ruins and azure seas. "The perfect setting for romance!" she says. "Rivaled only by the lush tropical heat of the Caribbean—palms swaying by a silver-sand beach lapped by turquoise waters... What more could lovers want?"

Books by Julia James

Harlequin Presents

Tycoon's Ring of Convenience
Billionaire's Mediterranean Proposal
Irresistible Bargain with the Greek
The Greek's Duty-Bound Royal Bride
The Greek's Penniless Cinderella
Cinderella in the Boss's Palazzo

One Night With Consequences

Heiress's Pregnancy Scandal

Visit the Author Profile page
at Harlequin.com for more titles.

Julia James

CINDERELLA'S BABY CONFESSION

HARLEQUIN
PRESENTS

HARLEQUIN®
PRESENTS®

Recycling programs
for this product may
not exist in your area.

ISBN-13: 978-1-335-56922-6

Cinderella's Baby Confession

Copyright © 2021 by Julia James

This edition published by arrangement with Harlequin Books S.A.

For questions and comments about the quality of this book,
please contact us at CustomerService@Harlequin.com.

Harlequin Enterprises ULC
22 Adelaide St. West, 40th Floor
Toronto, Ontario M5H 4E3, Canada
www.Harlequin.com

Printed in U.S.A.

CINDERELLA'S BABY CONFESSION

For my long-suffering editors,
JW and CT—they'll know why!

PROLOGUE

ALYS STARED AT the little white stick in her hand, blue line clearly visible. The blue line telling her that she was pregnant.

Pregnant.

The word tolled in her head, and she tightened her hand on the edge of the basin in the bathroom, as if to give herself strength.

How am I going to cope?

She dragged her gaze up to her reflection in the mirror over the basin. Her face was white with shock, eyes distended. Thoughts started to race through her head, urgent and fearful.

I can't be pregnant! I can't! Because I can't afford to be! Not now!

She felt a stab of fear claw at her. Downstairs on the kitchen table the letter that had fallen onto the doormat the previous morning still sat, its dread message stark in her head. She took a ragged breath, still staring at her stricken reflection.

Dear God, hadn't the last four years been hard enough? Ever since that nightmare day just before her finals, when she'd been phoned by one of her mother's colleagues to tell her that her mother was in the A&E department of the very hospital she worked in as a nurse. That she was being taken into emergency surgery after having been knocked down by a hit-and-run driver. That she might not survive surgery...

It was a phone call that had changed her mother's life—and hers.

Her mother had been made bedridden, almost entirely helpless, and had needed twenty-four-seven care—care that her daughter had given dedicatedly, devotedly, until complications from her horrendous injuries had finally led to her protracted death little more than six months ago.

Alys shut her eyes, head bowed, as if bearing too great a weight.

She had loved her mother, had willingly devoted herself to her care—but, oh, it had been hard! Hard to give up her own life, her own dreams, to care for her frail, broken-bodied mother—the mother who had devoted her life to the care of others suddenly needing total care herself. There had been times when Alys had longed to escape, to seize life with her own hands—but she had known she couldn't abandon her mother...

And when the end had come it had devastated her. Her mother, the only person in the world who had existed for her, who had loved her, was gone...

I've got no one—no one at all.

The bleak words that had been echoing in her head since her mother had died echoed again now.

Then without conscious thought she let the white stick with its fateful blue stripe fall into the basin. Let her hand drop and fold across the still completely slender curve of her midriff. She felt emotion well up within her. Her fingers splayed out, encompassing. Protective. Cherishing.

She *did* have someone—someone to love and be loved by. Invisible, intangible, beneath her splayed fingers. And suddenly, out of nowhere, it was not just a blue line on a stick, changing her life for ever, but something hugely, powerfully real.

My baby.

Emotion poured through her.

Whatever it takes, I'll do it! My baby will be safe and loved! I'll make a good home for it—somehow...

But she knew, with a hollow feeling inside her, just what that 'whatever it takes' would have to be.

And then memory came, vivid and unforgettable...

CHAPTER ONE

THE MUSIC FROM the DJ's deck pounded as Alys danced unenthusiastically with whoever it was she was dancing with—a friend of Suze, who was a friend of Maisey, whom Alys knew from uni days.

Maisey had urged her to come and stay with her in London for a weekend break—a break from the grim reality of probate, mortgage arrears and piercing grief—to come to this party tonight.

'It's some kind of flash bash at a luxury West End hotel that Suze has got invites for through her modelling contacts. It'll do you good! After all you've been through, a fabulous party is just what you need, hon!'

But now, having let Maisey lend her an outfit, do her hair and face, Alys was not so sure. Maybe she'd been out of circulation for too long, or maybe this kind of party was just not her thing. But she could feel male eyes on her, taking in the short tight dress, the wildly flowing long blonde hair, her eyes huge with make-up, her mouth made a rich scarlet with lipstick. And instead of enjoying herself she just wanted to cut and run, feeling totally out of it.

When the track finally ended, she headed back towards the cocktail lounge, intent on finding Suze, or Maisey, to tell them she was leaving. Her gaze threaded the room, searching for them...

And stopped dead.

As did the breath in her lungs.

Nikos stood by the bar, martini glass in hand, surveying the crowded room with displeasure. His mood was not good. He'd flown in from Brussels late that afternoon, having had to give Irinia her *congé* over lunch. It wasn't convenient to part with her—he had no replacement lined up as yet—but her increasingly blatant hints as to how their relationship could progress to their becoming engaged had passed the limit of his endurance. So he'd wished her well in her glittering career at one of Europe's international banks, and told her marriage was not on his agenda.

His dark eyes were shadowed in his strongly planed face. It hadn't always been so. Ten years ago he'd been engaged, desperate to marry. He'd been a gullible, trusting, eager-to-love twenty-two-year-old who'd naively believed the woman he'd fallen for loved him only for himself...

His sensual mouth twisted. It had been his father who'd saved him from making the worst mistake of his life. He could hear his words now.

'I had to threaten to disinherit you to get you to realise that Miriam Kapoulou only wanted to marry you so that Drakis money could stop her father going bankrupt!'

Miriam handing back his ring had proved his father right. As ever. He heard his father's words again.

'I won't let what happened to me happen to you! No gold-digging harpy will get her claws into you—whatever tricks she pulls!'

Nikos dragged his mind away. He'd grown up with the sorry saga of his own existence drummed into him all his life. Grown up with his father's perpetually resentful gaze on him…

Wishing to hell that I was any woman's son but the one who trapped him into marriage.

No, he wouldn't let his mood worsen by going over ground that was as painful as it was tediously familiar. He'd spent his boyhood trying to dispel that resentful gaze, spent his adulthood proving that he was a true Drakis. Doing what a Drakis did best in life. Making money.

And he was good at it—even his father had to acknowledge that. Deals came naturally to him and he could negotiate down to the wire. Thanks to his efforts, the Drakis coffers were overflowing. It was how he spent his life—on the move, with little time for leisure or relaxing. And when he did relax, it was not at hectic parties like this.

He was only here because he'd been expecting to

meet up with a City acquaintance who'd seen him checking in and casually invited him along this evening to a party he was hosting—something to do with the fashion industry, it would seem, given the preponderance of over-made-up model-types and fashionistas swanning around extravagantly.

Nikos's gaze swept over them disparagingly. Too many of them were here to pull, he suspected cynically—as were, concomitantly, the males as well, of course. Well, he wasn't going to be one of them. Not tonight. Not his style.

He surveyed the room, impatient to spot his City acquaintance and sound him out briefly, decide whether to follow up any potentially lucrative ventures with him.

And out of nowhere all thoughts of *Not tonight. Not my style* evaporated totally.

Alys stood, her gaze fastened as though pulled by a magnet to the man sitting at the bar on the far side of the crowded cocktail lounge. Tall, lean-bodied, dark-haired, thirtyish, with a tanned skin tone that spoke of Mediterranean climes and sculpted features that somehow made her think that she had never, in all her life, ever seen a man so lethally good-looking...

And he was looking right at her.

It was electrifying.

Unconsciously, she felt her lips part, her pulse quicken, as her eyes met his gaze across the room.

Then, distractingly, her former dance partner was helping himself to her wrist.

'Hey, babe, come on back!'

She turned, trying to tug herself free. 'No! Thank you—no!'

She got no further. Another voice—deep, accented and commanding—interjected. 'She said no.'

Alys's head spun round. It was the man from the bar, suddenly there, eyeballing her wannabe dance partner.

The restraining hand dropped from her wrist. 'OK, pal, I didn't know she was with you.'

'Well, now you do,' came the dismissive reply.

Alys felt her elbow lightly cupped, and then the man whose lethal good looks had stopped her totally in her tracks was guiding her towards the bar. She tried to pull her ragged thoughts together and failed totally. Instead, she let herself be helped onto a bar stool as the man settled himself back on his in a lithe movement.

'You look like you could do with a drink,' he said to her.

There was amusement in his voice now, the note of implacable command gone. She looked across at him, conscious that her heart was thumping, her pulse throbbing. Dear God, he really was the most fantastic-looking man she had seen in her life...

It was the eyes—incredibly dark, long-lashed, looking at her with a glint of amusement in them—

and also something much more. Something that told Alys, with an instinct as old as time, that he had not just intervened out of masculine chivalry.

That something else had motivated him.

That he was liking what he was seeing…liking it *a lot*…

She felt heat flare in her cheeks again, beneath the make-up Maisey had cheerfully slapped on her, and was grateful it was helping to subdue the colouring of her face under his gaze.

'So what would you like to drink?'

The accented voice came again, and she was glad of the enquiry.

'Um…a Sea Breeze?' she heard herself say, her voice somehow breathy, which it never normally was. But her breathing was too rapid, too shallow, her pulse-rate too hectic, for it to be anything else.

I was going to leave. Find Maisey and head off. And instead—

Instead she was perched on a bar stool, while a man who was like no other she'd ever set eyes on in her life was coolly presenting her with a just-mixed Sea Breeze, lifting his martini glass to her.

'Yammas,' he murmured.

Joltingly, her fingers closed around the icy column of her own glass, her scarlet-painted nails vivid against it, matching the cranberry-red of her cocktail.

'Yammas?' she heard herself say, glancing up at him.

A half-smile tugged at his mouth—one that did yet more damage to Alys's frail hold on normality.

'Greek for cheers,' he replied, and took a mouthful of his martini.

His eyes washed over her almost casually, as if mentally assessing her. Cataloguing her features.

Alys was burningly conscious of what he was seeing. Her mane of artfully tussled blonde hair rippled over her shoulders, her eyes were deep with shadow, lashes thick with mascara, mouth lush with lipstick. The dress Maisey had smoothed over her was tight, almost a size too small, and her breasts were crushed beneath it, exposing a curve of decolletage that she'd never exposed even in her uni days. The hem she was suddenly so conscious of was riding on her thighs, moulding them and the curve of her hip.

Instinctively she crossed her legs, hoping it would make the dress less tight. All it achieved, she realised, with a little frisson, was making that dark gaze flicker to her legs…

'Greek?' she heard herself say, as if that might draw the too-attentive flicker away from the short hem.

It succeeded, and his gaze returned to her face, veiled slightly beneath lashes that were surely too long for a mere male…

She saw him relax his stance, lay a casually placed forearm on the surface of the bar as he took another ruminative mouthful of his martini. Then he placed his glass back on the bar, holding out his hand instead.

'Nikos,' he said. 'Nikos Drakis.'

Giving his name made his accent more pronounced. There was something about the way he said it that for a second made Alys think he was expecting some response to his name. But what it was she had no idea.

'Alys,' she said, sliding her hand into his. 'Alys Fairford.'

It was the briefest contact, but she felt her cheeks flare again, her eyes going to him, meeting his. Mingling.

'Good to meet you, Alys. The evening was looking very tedious. But now...'

The low murmured voice was still infused with that faint amusement...and something more.

Something that banished, as if they had never existed, the four long, anguished years she had spent looking after her mother, locked away from the world, turning her back on anything else, denying herself everything the world might offer, feeling her youth slipping by...

Something that made her want, with a fierce longing, all that she had been denied. All that she was not going to deny any longer, with this incredible man looking at her the way he was, with those dark, irresistible eyes, as no man had ever looked at her before.

And the certainty was suddenly searing within her.

She was not going to deny it tonight.

There was a voice trying to make itself heard inside Nikos's head. Demanding what the hell he was thinking of, picking up one of this gilded flock of party girls thronging the place.

Responding to whatever it was that had drawn him to his feet, to remove her from the oaf pestering her, had been an impulse he couldn't explain. Didn't want to. He wanted only to let his eyes run over her, from that silken mane of artfully tousled hair, to the short hem of her dress, exposing those long slender legs.

Yet there was something about her that was more than her looks…

Maybe it was in the eyes. They were blue-grey and widened now, fastening on him with something in them that just for a moment gave him pause, that was somehow at odds with the rest of the packaging. Not that he objected to the packaging. Not in the least…

He resumed his full-on appreciation of her stunning physical charms. Male response as old as time started to purr within him as he went back to appreciating all that was on display. Though blatantly picking up an unknown female like the way he was doing now was not his habit, for a woman like this one he'd make an exception…

Unwelcome memory flickered in him. The all too familiar saga of his father's resentment-fuelled youth, and the woman who had so fatefully—so disastrously—caught his eye.

Nikos shook it from him. He wouldn't be making the same mistake his father had. Forewarned was forearmed.

He made himself relax, take another mouthful of his martini. This knock-out female had walked into his vision, so why not enjoy it? Enjoy the evening and, if she were like-minded, the night ahead too...

Would she be like-minded?

Dressed as she was, she looked as if he might have little doubt of it, and yet once again he felt that sense of contradiction, difference. He put it down to the wide-eyed expression with which she was so openly gazing at him. As if she just could not stop looking.

She dropped her gaze back to her cocktail tumbler, two spots of colour suddenly burning in her cheeks beneath a layer of make-up. That, too, didn't quite go with the glitzy packaging...

He set down his martini glass with a click. Time to make the next move. He smiled across at her. Warm and inviting. Gaze lambent. Lids half drooping.

'Have dinner with me, Alys,' he said.

The hotel restaurant was quiet, and Alys was glad of it. After the crowded cocktail lounge and the thudding dance floor, the hushed ambience of the Michelin-starred restaurant was welcome.

Am I really here?

That sense of dazed disbelief that had washed over her ever since she'd set eyes on the man who was now wining and dining her came over her again. But it was a disbelief that was becoming more and more real with every moment. Her other self, so long buried, so long suppressed, was riding higher and higher. A sense of recklessness—of being unleashed, of seizing everything that life had denied her for four long years—was taking her over. And she was welcoming it, embracing it, with every passing moment in the company of this fabulous man.

Is this really happening?

But the exquisite gourmet meal was deliciously real enough, and the way Nikos's dark, long-lashed gaze flickered over her was even more real, making her shiver inside with a response that came from deep within her.

They were conversing, and she was grateful she was able to carry on even a semblance of ordinary conversation when she could feel a shivering sense of awareness all through her, when her blood seemed to be throbbing in her veins and she could not stop it—did not want to.

She lifted a forkful of rich *canard au cassis*, asking him about his travels. He'd told her he was on the move constantly as part of his business, which seemed to be something about high finance and global investments—things she knew nothing about. But the question she asked was about the places in the world he'd been to—places she would never get to, and even if she did it would only ever be as a budget holiday traveller.

'The places I go to are less exciting than you'd think, Alys,' he was saying now. 'Brussels, Frankfurt, Geneva—all just places where business is done. So are places like New York, Shanghai and Sydney when you've been there more times than you can remember—and when you mostly just see the airport, a hotel and someone else's office! I don't get much time off.'

She paused in eating, looking across at him. He sounded jaded—almost…bitter?

'So why work so much?' she asked.

A thin smile was her reply. 'Contrary to popular opinion, money doesn't grow on trees.'

Alys frowned. 'But if you have enough for your needs, why go on making more?'

He picked up his wine glass, sitting back and looking at her with a slightly strange look in his eyes. 'How much money would you say you need, Alys?'

She blinked. 'Well, enough to pay the bills and a bit over, I suppose.' She gave a small shrug. 'I'm the wrong person to ask, really. I've always had to live modestly.' Even as she spoke she felt a twinge of guilt at eating a meal that she could never afford on her own… She bit her lip, feeling awkward. 'I'm sorry. Here I am, having this absolutely gorgeous gourmet meal…' Her voice trailed off.

The strange look in his eyes vanished, and his gaze was warming instead. 'You're more than welcome, Alys. After all, I did invite you, didn't I?'

She nodded, feeling better about it. But not entirely. Maybe it had been a mistake to accept his invitation to dinner…knowing what had motivated it. She reached for her wine, then hesitated. It was likely from a hideously expensive bottle.

She felt the lightest of touches at her wrist. 'Alys, I have said—you're my guest. Enjoy!'

Her eyes met his. In his there was only warmth. She felt the tension leave her. All the same, she wanted to move on to a safer topic.

She took a sip of her wine, then set the glass back on the table. 'So, if all you ever see of those fantastic countries you fly to is the airport, a hotel and offices, what about your own homeland?' Her voice warmed. 'I've never been to Greece—is it as beautiful as it looks? All those Aegean islands!'

'I don't travel about in Greece much. I'm based in Athens. There's a family villa on one of the islands, but I can't remember when I was last there.'

'Oh, that's a shame!' she said spontaneously. She directed a little smile at him. 'You should definitely promise yourself a visit soon. Take some time off! Chillax!'

'In the right company, that might sound appealing…'

His voice was distinctly husky, and Alys felt her cheeks warm. She reached for her wine again and then went on eating. A sudden, disturbingly intimate vision assailed her, of her and Nikos basking on the beach outside a beautiful Greek villa…

She was glad when he moved the subject on. 'So what about you, Alys? Are you a Londoner?'

She shook her head. 'I'm staying with an old uni friend at the moment. Home is in the Midlands. A rather dull dormitory town near Birmingham—though there is lovely countryside around. And it's not too far from Stratford-upon-Avon.'

That was safer territory, and she was glad when he followed up on it, talking about Shakespeare. Her voice warmed with enthusiasm as she recalled productions seen in her student days, which led on to him talking about classical Greek theatre.

She joined in readily, finding him both knowledgeable and easy to talk to. It was heady, knowing that she could talk so easily to someone whose incredible looks could make her melt inside—as if she had known him for much longer than a bare hour or two. He was putting her at her ease, and she was aware of that, yet she couldn't help but respond to it.

At some point she became aware he was eyeing her curiously. 'You realise I'd thought you were something in the fashion industry?' he said. 'With your looks, maybe a model?'

She felt herself colouring again slightly. 'Oh, no, I'm not tall enough—or thin enough!'

He lifted his wine glass, taking a leisurely mouthful, resting his eyes on her. 'I wouldn't change a thing about you, Alys,' he replied.

And that husky sound was there in his voice again.

As was the colour in her cheeks.

And the quickening of her heartbeat when he looked at her like that, with those incredibly dark deep eyes of his…

He tilted his wine glass to her. 'To you, Alys— and to our evening together…'

His eyes held hers and she could not let hers drop—could not do anything except fall into his expressive gaze, which was telling her burningly, clearly, just why she was with him…

Then he was speaking again.

'I only regret that I have to fly out tomorrow,' he said, and the huskiness was gone now, leaving something brisker in his voice instead. 'Geneva. I'm only passing through London briefly.'

He met her eyes, and Alys got the impression he was conveying something to her. For a moment she didn't know what. Then she did. It made her flush, and reach for her wine glass. She said nothing, and a moment later he had gone on to make some re-mark comparing Geneva to Zurich, drawing more questions from her about both, and the conversation moved on in the same easy fashion as before.

Yet all the time another conversation was running. She knew it, felt it—did not reject it. And when, at the end of their leisurely, exquisite meal, it finally surfaced, she did not reject it then either.

He sat back, idly cupping the bowl of his empty wine glass, resting his half-hooded gaze on her, giving nothing away—giving *everything* away.

'Shall we have coffee upstairs?' he murmured.

He paused, and the expression in his eyes told her that the question he was asking her was more than those words.

'What do you say, Alys?'

She could feel her heart beating beneath the tight contours of her dress. Feel the supreme consciousness of the moment.

This won't come again. If I say no now he'll smile, and accept my answer, and see me into a taxi. He'll thank me for the evening...and it will all be over...

And she couldn't bear this amazing, intoxicating encounter with this fabulous man to be over—not yet.

She heard her own voice speak. Give him the answer that he wanted—that she did too.

'Why not?' she replied.

And felt her heart beat more strongly than ever.

CHAPTER TWO

CAREFULLY, NIKOS LEVERED himself out of bed, then stood looking down at the slender, still-sleeping figure half covered by the bedclothes, pale hair drifting across the pillows. A frown drew his brows together. She looked so different from the way she'd looked the evening before.

At some point in the night she must have retired to the en suite bathroom and removed her layers of make-up, because her face was quite clear of it— as were her eyes. No longer heavily shadowed, her eyelids were almost translucent, and her lashes, without lashings of mascara, spiked delicately on her cheek.

His frown deepened. She looked younger. More…innocent.

He discarded the word. Discarded, too, the memories that pricked at him now of the way she'd gone into his arms, with passion flaring in her eyes, her lips receiving his, opening to him as he'd drawn her enticing body against his.

And yet for all her readiness to return his ardency there had been that last-minute hesitation as he had led her into the suite's bedroom. He'd kissed her again, consumingly and deeply, sweeping her up into his arms to lower her down upon the bed, peeling her too-tight dress from her, eager to feast on the lissom body beneath that had been tempting him all evening and which he could no longer resist.

Could that hesitation have been shyness? Or had she merely been being coy?

At the time he hadn't cared—his arousal had been full and he'd wanted only to sate it, and to bring her to the pleasure he knew he could arouse in her. Memory flared again, hot and humid. And he had brought it to her time and time again.

Now, as he looked down at her, he felt arousal stir again. There had been something about his possession of her, hers of him… She'd clutched him to her, her fingertips indenting on his shoulders, her slender thighs holding his fast as her spine had arched beneath him, and her face had lit like a living flame as her body pulsed and throbbed around him, enclosing him in a union of the flesh that had been…

Like nothing I have known.

Again, that frown flickered in his eyes, as if seeking questions he did not wish to answer, only to suppress.

He clenched his jaw with a fierce imposition of necessary self-control, and had to suppress the overpowering urge to lower himself beside her once more, to turn her sleeping form to his and wake her in the way that he so wanted to...

He turned away—forced himself to do so. There was no time for anything more than what he had had already. His morning schedule was full, and then, as he had deliberately warned her, he was flying out to Geneva.

He strode into the bathroom, decisively shutting the door. She'd come out of nowhere, for one night only, and whether his impulse to keep her with him for the night had been rash or irresistible, it was, without a doubt, now over.

Alys stirred, waking slowly from sleep. Nikos was kissing her. But not as he had kissed in the long, endless night... This was brief, not lingering. A token kiss, no more than that.

She opened her eyes and saw him straightening away from her, standing by the bed, fully dressed, as he had been the night before, in a business suit. He was freshly showered and shaved, with a faint hint of expensive aftershave about him, and the morning light was glinting on gold cufflinks.

He smiled down at her, but it was not the intimate, sensual smile of their lovemaking. It was a smile that hinted of regret and dismissal—no more than that. Making it clear to her that their time together, so brief, was now over.

'I have to leave,' he told her. 'There's no rush

for you,' he went on. 'Take all the time you want. Order breakfast, obviously—it's on the suite's tab.' He paused, still looking down at her. 'I want you to know,' he went on, and now she could hear the faintest huskiness in his deep voice, 'how very memorable our night together was.'

For an instant so brief it almost seemed not to exist, he seemed to hesitate. Then it was gone. He smiled again, but his eyes were still veiled. All intimacy vanished.

'Look after yourself, Alys,' he said.

Then he was turning away, walking out of the bedroom. A moment later she heard the suite door open and close again. Then there was silence. She was alone.

Alone with only golden memories of a night that would never—could never—come again in her life. A night that would change her life for ever.

Three months later

Nikos gazed out of the window over the wide Atlantic far below, stretching out his legs in the spacious first-class seat as the plane headed east. It would land at Schiphol in the morning, the familiar red-eye, and there in the Netherlands he'd change planes and head south, back to Athens, ready to debrief his father on another lucrative business venture accomplished, boosting Drakis profits yet higher.

His father would be pleased.

'You're proving yourself a true Drakis!'

He could already hear his father's approbation. And something else. Something that always edged his father's voice when he spoke to him. Something that always grated.

Deliberately, he flicked his thoughts away, lifting the glass of pre-dinner champagne to his mouth. His negotiations in Chicago had been tough, requiring focussed concentration and days of late-night working. What he wanted now, he knew, was some R&R.

And he knew just who with...

The fantastic blonde who'd beguiled him that night in London when he'd finished with Irinia.

He frowned. He'd tried telling himself it had been a one-off indulgence—an impulse he couldn't explain and didn't need to. Yet since that night he hadn't been able to put her out of his mind. Or his memory.

She flickered there now, just as beguilingly as if she were actually with him. The memory of her velvet mouth opening to his, the sweet ripeness of her breasts cupped in his hand, her body arching to receive his...

He set down his champagne glass with a click. This wasn't the place for such memories. But they filled his head all the same.

He hadn't given her any indication that they would have any more than a single night together.

After all, unlike Irinia, she didn't come from his world. He had picked her up at a party, seduced her that very evening, never intending it to be any more than a passing fancy.

But why shouldn't I make it more?

They'd been good together—*very* good.

Memorable—that was what he'd said to her that morning when he'd left her lying in his bed.

So why deny himself something that had been that good? He'd wanted her from the first moment he'd set eyes on her.

And I still do.

He reached for his champagne again, decision made. He wouldn't go straight back to Athens after all. He'd divert via London.

Find Alys.

Make her his once more.

Sunshine bathed the little garden beyond the kitchen window, but Alys could not appreciate it. She'd received a second official notification—more starkly worded than the first—informing her that unless payment of her mortgage arrears were received, court proceedings would start imminently.

Foreclosure.

The grim word tolled in her head and real fear clutched at her. This modest semi had been her home since her schooldays, when her mother had finally saved enough money to put down a deposit, start paying a mortgage instead of rent. She had managed to raise her single-handedly, somehow juggling a baby, a child, then a teenager, with the non-stop demands of being a hospital nurse.

How much of her mother had she actually seen during her childhood?

Not enough.

That was the brutality of it.

I don't want that for my baby.

But what she did want—desperately—was a safe home, first and foremost.

Fear clutched at her again. To be threatened with losing her home now, of all times, with a baby on the way…

The mortgage company had allowed the arrears to build up after her mother's accident, switching to interest-only repayments, which had just been manageable with her mother's incapacity benefit and Alys's carer's allowance, and a great deal of punishing, penny-pinching budgeting. But after her mother's death payment of the backdated monthly repayments had been demanded.

Alys had begged for more time and got a job— nothing fancy, just something in the nearby super- market—before making a start on the mountain of arrears. But now repayment in full was being de- manded. Foreclosure was threatened.

Alys looked out through the window over the sunlit garden, which was mocking her with its brightness.

There was only one way to get the kind of money she needed in time—only one hope.

She bit her lip, her expression stark. The letter she'd sent—so difficult to write, so essential—had been posted to the hotel in London, with a request to forward it.

But would it be forwarded?

And, even if it was, how would Nikos respond?

She simply had no idea.

Nikos walked across the hotel lobby, heading for the concierge desk. Concierges knew everything that went on at a hotel, and he was the man most likely to be able to track down the woman who had been at a hotel function several months ago.

'Ah, Mr Drakis—how good to see you again. What can we do for you this evening?'

The familiar greeting of the concierge was reassuring. But, on the point of making his enquiry, Nikos saw the man take something out of a drawer in his desk, hold it out to him.

'We were about to forward this on to you, sir,' the concierge said.

Nikos frowned, glancing at the envelope. He took it, noting the thin, cheap paper and the handwritten address—his name, care of the hotel. It had a UK stamp on it, but the postmark was blurred. His frown deepened and automatically he turned away, ripping open the envelope, impatient to dispose of whatever it held so that he could put his enquiry to the concierge.

But as his eyes scanned the handwritten contents that enquiry became totally and absolutely unnecessary... As did all his plans for the woman who had beguiled him that single memorable night. And who had just exploded a bomb in his life.

Alys finished her last piece of toast and put her plate in the sink. She needed to get going...head down to the supermarket for her shift. Her mood was bleak. The morning's post had been and gone, and there was still nothing from Nikos.

What if he just doesn't want to know?

After all, it would hardly be welcome news, would it?

Her expression changed, became haunted by a familiar ghost. One that had been with her all her childhood.

Her mother's words rang in her ears.

'I never told him—he wouldn't have wanted to know, believe me...'

A pang smote her—an old grief, a sense of loss for the father she had never known, who had never known about her. She took a breath, her hand going to her midriff. At least *her* baby would never have to bear hearing *her* say, *I never told him...*

Then her burst of defiance collapsed. She might have written to tell Nikos that she was going to have his baby—but that didn't mean he intended acknowledging it. Let alone helping her financially.

The stab of too-familiar fear came again, at the threat of foreclosure hanging over her head, and even as it did so she heard the front door bell ring. It was a courier, holding out an envelope to her.

'Needs to be signed for,' the courier announced, and proffered an electronic pen and pad.

She closed the door after signing, ripping open the envelope anxiously. Was this the possession order she was dreading?

Please, no.

But the single sheet of paper was not from the mortgage company.

It was from Nikos.

And as she read it relief flooded through her.

The plane was starting its descent. Out of the window Alys could see the coast of Greece, so familiar from maps, with the narrow isthmus of Corinth leading out from the mountainous mainland into the bulge of the Peloponnese.

Memory plucked at her of how she'd asked questions of Nikos about his homeland that night she'd had dinner with him—the night he'd swept her into his bed. The night that had brought her here, now, flying out after using the plane ticket Nikos had provided, having dug out her passport, unused since student days, filled with relief that he was not rejecting the news that she was pregnant from their single night together.

Because why else would he have sent for her?

She felt the plane dip, drop height, and pressed her hand down on the arm of the seat, feeling her stomach drop too. Would Nikos be there, at the airport, waiting to greet her as she came out at Arrivals?

Thoughts raced through her head—thoughts that should not be there, that had no place there. They swept her back to that night when he had only had to smile at her, only had to let his lidded gaze wash over her to make her feel she was melting honey...

She wiped away such tempting memories with a shake of her head. She had not come here to see Nikos again as a lover—that single night they'd shared was all he'd wanted of her. She had to accept that. After all, he'd made no mention of seeing her again, of their encounter being anything more than what it had been. She'd never heard from him since—only now, in response to the letter she had sent him telling him about the baby. The baby that, thankfully, it seemed he was prepared to acknowledge.

Neither of us intended this to happen, but now it has surely we can sort out something between us...

She felt anxiety nip at her again. Whatever the eventual outcome of what she and Nikos agreed to, surely he would not want to see her made homeless?

As for anything more—would he want any involvement other than financial? She must not hope too much. Must not impose the forlorn hopes of her own fatherless childhood on him...

With a change in engine note and ailerons lowering, the plane glided down towards the runway that seemed to race up to meet the wheels. There was the bump of contact, the roar of reverse thrust—and she had arrived in Athens.

To whatever awaited her here.

Her fate, and that of the baby she carried.

Nikos glanced at his watch. The plane would have landed now, and Alys would be en route to the city in the car he'd sent for her, taking her to the hotel he'd booked her into. Nowhere fashionable—the last thing he wanted was anyone seeing him with her, starting gossip. His expression hardened. There would be gossip aplenty before long. Unless...

No, he would not give space to such pointless thoughts. He would deal with the situation as it developed, on the basis of fact, not speculation.

Forcibly, he dropped his eyes to the complex document he was perusing, which set out the intricate terms and conditions of the latest deal his father had assigned him to. After this one was com-

plete there would be another one for him to land.
And then another. It was his life—deal-making.

A true Drakis! Those words were what his father would praise him with.

His mouth twisted in bitter irony. Soon he would be striking a different kind of deal. One he would have no choice but to strike.

Unless…

That word again! He dismissed it, as he had before, forcing his gaze to focus on the fine print in front of him on the wide mahogany desk in his palatial office in the splendid edifice that had been Drakis HQ for over a hundred years—a historic heritage which, so his father constantly informed him, he was fortunate to possess. To strive to be worthy of…

Father to son for over a hundred years.

Even a son like himself—

He pulled his mind away. What point to dwell on what had been drummed into him all his life? None. Except that now, irony of bitter ironies—

No! With a clenching of his fist he silenced his jibing thoughts. By sheer willpower he focussed finally on the document in front of him. Time enough tomorrow to face what must be faced.

Alys was standing to one side of the lobby in the hotel she had been delivered to by the civil but unforthcoming driver who had held up her name as she'd emerged into Arrivals and ushered her into a sleek, expensive-looking car with tinted windows, that had purred quietly as it made its way from the airport into the city.

She had craned her neck, trying to take in her surroundings, burningly conscious that her stomach was still hollow, that she was truly here in Greece.

Summoned by Nikos Drakis.

Of whom there had been no sign—at the hotel or thereafter. Only a message, relayed to her by the receptionist, to say that she would be called for the following morning at eleven o'clock.

She had been given her room key, and her small suitcase had been removed by a bellhop who had escorted her to a room in this modern but quite anonymous hotel. She'd felt her spirits, determinedly buoyed up during the flight, sink right down. Tiredness had swept over her, for the day had been long, and stressful—the coach journey to London, then the tube out to Heathrow and the four-hour flight to Athens.

Now, the next day, waiting in the lobby a few minutes before eleven, her back and shoulders stiff, she saw the same driver who had brought her from the airport walking into the lobby. He came up to her, bidding her follow him. She did so, clutching her handbag, and he opened the rear passenger door of an even sleeker, more expensive-looking car than yesterday's, which was waiting at the kerb.

She climbed inside the spacious interior.

Nikos was there on the far side, his face un-smiling.

CHAPTER THREE

NIKOS'S EYES WENT to her. His first thought was that he barely recognised her. She couldn't have looked more different from the way she had that night in London. Her hair was drawn back into a tight French pleat, she had not a scrap of make-up on, and her plain shirt dress in pale brown obviously came from a chain store.

His gaze dropped automatically to her midriff. Absolutely nothing showed.

Memory—completely illogical, completely inappropriate—suddenly pierced Nikos's armour-plated thoughts.

A memory of how he'd first set eyes on her, paused in the cocktail lounge, drawing his gaze towards her for reasons he still could not explain to himself. His eyes lingering on her...how incredibly, irresistibly enticing she'd looked...

His already thin lips thinned even more.

Well, I damn well should have resisted her!
But it was too late for regrets.
Far too late.

Alys sat back in the deep, soft leather seat. Her mouth had gone dry and she could think of nothing to say. Thoughts of what she might have been expecting from Nikos—hoping for—had disappeared.

Then Nikos spoke. Just saying her name.

She swallowed, then gave an awkward half-nod, wondering how best to respond to that unsmiling face.

'Thank you for inviting me here,' she got out. It seemed the only thing to say.

'What else did you expect?' Nikos's voice was as dry as it was accented. He nodded at her. 'You will need to do up your seat belt,' he informed her.

Thankful for something to occupy her, she fumbled with the belt, finally getting it slotted into place. She was burningly aware that, despite his unnerving, unsmiling gaze, he was having exactly the same impact on her as the first time she'd set eyes on him—he had the same lethal good looks, the same potent air of cosmopolitan elegance in his superbly tailored light grey business suit, the same hint of expensive-smelling aftershave, familiar from spending that one and only night in his arms.

But she must not think of that—not now. The car was moving off into the traffic, and she glanced out through the car's window.

'Where...where are we going?' She tried to make her voice sound normal, but knew it wasn't.

'To get you checked out,' came the reply.

The accented voice was cool, completely unlike the warmth that had been in it at their first encounter.

Our only encounter.

'Checked out?' Her gaze swivelled back to Nikos.

'A medical check-up at an obstetrics clinic.'

'Oh. I had a check-up last week. At my GP surgery, with the midwife—'

'This will be far more thorough,' Nikos cut across her. 'With a consultant obstetrician.'

She fell silent. Her thoughts were in tumult. She hadn't known what to expect when she met Nikos again, how he would react. Well, now she knew. And she could feel her heart sink.

Impulsively, she spoke again. 'Nikos, I know this has come as a shock to you. It did to me. I never expected—'

She broke off. For a moment he simply held her gaze, his own totally unreadable. She turned away again, looking out of her tinted window, dismay spiking through her.

I shouldn't have come! I should never have written that letter to him telling him about the baby—

She cut herself off mid-flow, her lips pressing tightly. It was too late for regrets—and anyway, she thought silently, she couldn't afford to regret telling him. The threatening letter from the mortgage company weighed like lead in the base of her handbag.

She heard Nikos start to say something, but as she turned her head she realised it wasn't to her. He'd taken out his phone and was making a phone call. It was in Greek, and she was glad of it, turning her head away again, tension racking her.

The tension stayed for the rest of the car journey, until the car pulled up outside a modern building, and the driver got out, opening her door. Nikos got out as well, and led the way inside, striding up to the reception desk and speaking tersely in Greek.

A nurse came hurrying forward and approached Alys, who was lingering by the door. 'Please come this way,' the nurse addressed Alys.

Alys half looked at Nikos, but he had settled himself down in the waiting area, was picking up a newspaper…ignoring her. Numbly, she followed the nurse, and was shown into a spacious consulting room.

'Ah, Miss Fairford—how very good to meet you!'

The urbane, dark-suited consultant behind the wide desk got to his feet, gesturing for her to be seated, and resumed his own seat, opening up the folder placed in front of him by the nurse, who then stood back, hands folded neatly, clearly 'in attendance'.

The obstetrician introduced himself, his English only slightly accented, and then smiled benignly. 'Now, before we proceed to the examination, may I just check the details so far? Is this your first pregnancy? Yes…good. And how many weeks would you say? I see. Any discomfort of any kind so far? No? Good…good. No medical issues? You've been seen by your own doctor, of course, and heard nothing but good? Excellent! Now, allow me to place you in the care of my nurse, and then we'll make ourselves absolutely certain that everything is proceeding exactly as it should.'

He smiled again, as warm and reassuring as only a very expensive medical consultant could be, and then left her with the nurse to supervise her undressing.

It was quite some time before she was ready to emerge again from the consulting room. Nikos had been right. It had been a very thorough check-up indeed.

And if there had been the slightest flicker in the consultant's eyes when she'd confirmed that she knew exactly how far her pregnancy had progressed, that there could be no ambiguity about the date of conception, she had refused to allow herself to blush.

Nikos Drakis was there that night with me!

And one night was all it had taken.

'Please come this way, Miss Fairford.'

The nurse was speaking again, and Alys was shown into a small, but comfortably appointed waiting room, with easy chairs, magazines on the table, washroom facilities and a complicated-looking coffee machine.

'Allow me to make you a coffee,' the nurse said brightly.

Alys nodded, wondering what was going to happen next. She had given the consultant her permission to talk to Nikos, answer any questions he might have, so presumably he was doing that now. She sipped her decaff, a troubled look on her face. Feeling very alone. And very far from home.

Nikos lowered himself into the chair in front of the obstetrician's desk.

'Well?' His demand was terse.

'Definitely pregnant. And, yes, she is as advanced as would be expected after what you have told me,' came the answer, smoothly spoken, professional and medically authoritative.

Nikos's expression did not change. Nor did he speak, only went on listening as the consultant briefed him, finishing by indicating the expected due date of Alys's eventual delivery shortly after Christmas.

The words echoed in Nikos's ears.

And then I will become a father...the father of a child...

Emotion scythed through him. Many emotions, all tumultous, had been doing so ever since that fateful moment when he had ripped open that cheap, thin envelope the hotel concierge had handed him. Yet none had had anything like the intensity of the one that possessed him now.

But he set it aside. He had no room for it yet, could not, must not, acknowledge it. Because there was another question he had to ask—could not, must not, avoid.

A question on which would hang the future of his life—and not just his own. A question he did not want to ask but must.

He eyeballed the consultant, looking back at him with his professionally bland expression, and put the question to him.

'All finished?'

The nurse had come in again, and was glancing at the half-drunk cup of coffee on the table by Alys.

'Mr Drakis is waiting for you in reception,' she informed her with a polite smile.

Thankful, Alys got to her feet, picking up her handbag, following the nurse out of the room.

Nikos's tall, severely suited figure struck her immediately as he stood up, clearly indeed waiting for her, with the same unsmiling expression on his face as before. He asked no questions of her, nor said anything, only ushered her from the clinic and back into the car that was waiting by the entrance.

Alys felt her own expression tighten, mirroring his as she resumed her seat. Could this brusque, unsmiling man really be the same man who had melted her with his desiring gaze, swept her into his arms, his bed…who had been sensual, seductive and, oh, so passionate towards her? Had that night really happened? It seemed almost unbelievable.

She felt emotion tug at her—a sense of desolation. This was not how she'd imagined it would be. Not by a million miles. Whatever she had hoped for, this was not it…

Then he was speaking, and she made herself pay attention as the car moved off.

'I'll drop you back at your hotel,' Nikos was saying, his voice as inexpressive as his face, his glance unrevealing. 'I suggest you rest in the afternoon. Tonight…' An edge had crept into his voice—Alys could hear it. 'Tonight we must talk. I'll send a car for you at eight. Please be ready in time,' he finished.

Alys said nothing. A moment later he'd got his phone out again and seemed to be checking emails.

She left him to it, turned to look out of her window but saw nothing, her thoughts bleak.

Out of nowhere, a sudden urge to tell Nikos to drive her to the airport—to send her back to England—almost overcame her. To tell him that *she* would deal with everything from now on, that he could absolve himself of all responsibility as to the reason she was here at all!

Then emotion twisted inside her, like a wire tightening around her guts, as she remembered the letter in her handbag.

She fought for composure. Nikos had said they would talk tonight. OK, so talk they would.

This is not just my baby! It's his too. So he has responsibilities as well as me!

Responsibilities that surely meant she had every right to ask him—a wealthy man, after all!—for the financial help she so urgently needed.

She felt her hands tighten over her handbag again.

He can't turn me down! Surely he can't.

That was the hope she had to cling to. However much she didn't want to.

Nikos was back in his office, attempting to work. But it was impossible. His mind was far too full. The arrival of his father, just walking in, was the last thing he needed.

'You were going to give me a progress report

on the New York deal—where is it?' his father demanded, not bothering with pleasantries.

'You'll get it—but not right now,' Nikos rejoined. He was in no mood for his father's browbeating.

'Later is no use,' his father barked back. 'Haven't I drummed into you that time is always of the essence? You have to close—and fast—every time. Don't ever let the other party have time to manoeuvre, rethink, get ideas, find alternative partners. As my son, you should know that by now!'

Dark eyes lanced Nikos, the expression in them one that had been familiar for so, so long.

Bitterness rose in Nikos's throat.

Always the same! The barbs—the resentment. The constant reminders about the son I 'should' be...

It had been that way all his life.

He hauled his mind away. He must not let it go there—not with his father standing right there in front of his desk, frowning in displeasure.

The stab of bitterness came again in Nikos's throat.

Because I can never, never be the son he wants—not with the mother I had.

He felt emotions swirl within him, dark and turbid. But they were not about himself. In his head he heard the obstetric consultant confirming Alys's pregnancy, and felt those turbulent emotions swirl inside him again, darker now. Memory bit—how he had warned himself, that fateful evening he'd first set eyes on her, to make sure he didn't go down the same dangerous path his own father had. How he'd arrogantly dismissed his own warning to himself.

Well, he was paying for it now, all right.

But I have to ensure that only I pay for it! Not—

He stilled his thoughts, crushing down the fierce emotions that went with them. His father was talking at him still, moving on, wanting reports on other deals in the pipeline, on fresh prospects on the Drakis agenda. An agenda that never got any shorter, that always had to be fulfilled, that kept Nikos globetrotting constantly. Because that was what being a Drakis was all about. As he constantly had to prove…

Teeth gritted, Nikos gave his father the updates he demanded, and it was a good hour later before he had his office to himself again. He glanced at his watch. No point trying to focus on business any longer. There was only one focus for him now.

The evening ahead.

And the woman he was going to have to spend it with.

And why.

Because it's the most important deal I'll ever make in my life.

And he could not—*could not*—afford to lose.

His eyes glittered darkly as he threw himself back in his leather chair. But why should he lose? He held the trump card—the one that would win every time. The one that, tonight, she would feel the full force of. Feel the full lure of.

Drakis money.

He stared blindly out across his spacious, thickly carpeted office, climate-controlled against the increasing heat of Athens as spring gave way to summer.

Tonight I will show her what can be hers.

Alys was asleep. Delayed exhaustion had wiped her out after she'd tried to consume the sandwich lunch delivered to her by room service, but now a knock at her door was rousing her. It was the bellhop, handing her a wide, flat, white-lacquered cardboard box, embellished with large gold lettering in Greek script she couldn't read.

Blinkingly, she took it, putting it down on her bed. A gilt envelope was tucked into the satin ribbon tying up the box, with a card inside it.

For you to wear tonight—Nikos

She lifted the glazed lid of the box, peeling aside the silver tissue paper to reveal a dress. A cocktail frock in slub silk, pale green, in a tailored, knee-length shift style, with darted bodice. It was sleeveless, with a round neckline, and very slightly fuller at the waist.

As she held it up, Alys's face lit with sheer pleasure at so beautiful a garment. A designer number, obviously, and it was impossible not to feel delight at holding it up to view.

And temptation too. She was honest enough to acknowledge it. When, in her life, had such a dress ever been within her reach? Never—that was the answer.

But for the mother of Nikos Drakis's child...?

The thought hovered in the air, tantalising and taunting. If she had not spent time with him today, seen him unsmiling, businesslike, the hopes that she had been harbouring might not have been wiped from her. Hopes for something even as modest as coming to a civil, amicable agreement between them. If she had only recalled how he'd been in London that magical evening, she would have still been filled with unquestioning delight at so beautiful a dress.

A sense of longing rose up in her. To make that unforgettable evening come again, to put on this beautiful, expensive dress for Nikos, to make herself as beautiful as she could for him, to see again that look in his eyes, desiring her...

She crushed it down, as pointless as it was impossible. Most likely, she thought bleakly, he'd only sent the dress because he didn't want to be seen dining with a woman in a cheap outfit like the one she'd worn today.

For a moment she was filled with an impulse to pack it away in its box again. Then she paused, her expression steeling. Maybe wearing an expensive dress like this, the indifferent offering of a rich man, would serve to remind her of just how rich he was—and how urgently, desperately, for her baby's sake, she needed him to be.

Nikos reached for the cocktail that had been placed in front of him as he'd taken his seat in the restaurant—one of Athens's most exclusive—and took a mouthful of the strong, astringent martini, feeling he could do with its shot to the system. Beneath his habitual impassiveness he could still feel that hard, heavy stone inside him. The one that had been there since his world had imploded. Since he'd read Alys's letter, telling him she was pregnant.

History repeating itself. First my father— now me.

Bitterness, on so many counts, was acid in his throat.

His phone pinged and he glanced down at it. His driver, informing him that he'd dropped Alys off. So she would be here imminently.

His eyes went to the restaurant entrance and she was there—being ushered unctuously towards him. Nikos's eyes fastened on her, and as they did so he knew, with a plunging hollowness inside him, that sending her that dress had been a mistake. A big mistake.

The emotions he'd had no intention of giving admittance to surged uncontrollably.

Thee mou, but she looks incredible!

He could not tear his eyes from her as she approached. If he'd been unable to resist her when she'd been looking so blatantly over-the-top and enticing that first fateful evening, now she was looking just…

Perfection. Absolute perfection. This is the way she should always look!

The image was flawless. The dress was ideal for her, flattering her fair colouring, and the ultra-chic simplicity of its design only enhanced the fullness of her natural beauty—a beauty subtly enhanced by the make-up widening her eyes, shaping her mouth, heightening her cheekbones. But nothing was overdone, like at that party, and nothing was unnecessarily slapped on. Her hair was not loose in wild abandon, as it had been that night, nor tightly pulled back as it had been this morning. Now it was loosely, gracefully coiled, wound around itself at the nape of her neck, accentuating the fine-boned contours of her face, the slender extent of her throat, exposing her tender earlobes.

He felt the visceral response of his body, and for a few abandoned moments let himself simply drink her in. Other male heads had turned as she'd crossed the restaurant floor, and he knew exactly why.

No wonder I could not resist her that night! No wonder I threw caution to the winds and made her mine!

His expression altered. Yes, he had—he had,

indeed. And now there was going to be a price to pay for it. Who better than himself to know that?

All my life.

It was like a douche of cold water in his veins.

His eyes hardened, veiling, and he got to his feet.

'Alys.' He kept his voice punctiliously civil, stayed standing until she was seated before resuming his own chair. His reaction to her was back under control, and his gaze flicked over her assessingly. But not just in respect of her beauty, however breathtaking. She was looking outwardly composed, but he could see a pulse beating at her throat. She was not as calm as she obviously wanted him to think.

He heard her murmur his name, then busy herself with her napkin. Waiters were there, placing menus in front of them, and the customary rituals of bringing iced water and bread rolls gave him time to dispense with the last echoes of his response to her. There was no place for it now. None.

The dress is to impress her—not me.

That was its purpose. Not to remind him of her fantastic beauty, or the impact it could have on him.

Yet for all his reminders he heard himself say, as the waiting staff finally took themselves off, 'The dress suits you.'

Had there been a trace of admiration in his voice? He strove to keep it nothing more than civil.

'Yes. Thank you for thinking of it,' Alys answered him, in the same unexceptional tones.

He saw her glance around, take in the elegance of her surroundings, including the other diners. Then her gaze came back to him, and he thought he saw something change in her eyes, but it was swiftly concealed.

It had been there for only a fraction of a second, but that was all that it had taken. Even less than the time it reached him. He slammed shut on it. It had no place here. Not now.

Waiters were hovering attentively, proffering menus, asking Alys what she would like to drink. She asked for orange juice and soda. Nikos found himself remembering how she'd ordered a Sea Breeze in London. But remembering anything about that fateful night was irrelevant. Only what he had to achieve now was of any purpose.

The most important deal of his life—

He flipped open his menu. 'Tell me, what might you like to eat tonight? This restaurant is noted for its soufflés. Does that appeal? Savoury as well as sweet.' He made his tone of voice civil. For now.

She glanced up from her menu. 'Whatever you think best.'

He could hear constraint still in her voice. There had been none that night he'd swept her off with him.

What if I could do that tonight?

The thought was in his head before he could stop it. Block it. Bringing in its wake more tumbling thoughts, just as out of place.

I intended to pick up with her again—have more time with her. So why not?

Again he slammed down hard on his thoughts. Whatever he'd once intended had vanished the moment he'd read her letter. Now there was only one priority. And it was *not* the way she looked right now and what it was doing to him.

His eyes went to her, focussing on the only important thing about her now. She did not look pregnant—had the obstetrician not confirmed it, he would not have believed it. And yet...

Is there something about her that is not just the elegance of her dress, her natural beauty?

He wanted to rest his eyes on her but did not permit himself. He had an agenda for tonight—and he would stick to it. And it did *not* entail memories that no longer had any use. Or intentions that were long gone and could not come back. The present was all that mattered. Succeeding in his purpose.

The waiter was there again, setting down her juice, taking their food order before disappearing again. Nikos turned down the wine menu—he wanted a completely clear head...one martini was enough. He took another mouthful, then set down his glass.

Time to open the dealing.

'So, Alys,' he said, and his eyes rested on her with deliberate unreadability, 'let's talk. Just what is it that you want?'

CHAPTER FOUR

ALYS STILLED. So here it was, then. The purpose of her presence here—the reason she had come to Greece, had contacted Nikos at all. She lifted her chin, steeling herself to say what she had to say. She would make it clear to him, however difficult it was.

However much I wish it wasn't like this—that you were like you were in London. Not this cold, unsmiling stranger, so obviously unwelcoming of my presence here, and the reason for it.

She took a breath, making herself look right at him, unflinchingly. 'Nikos, I don't have to be a mind-reader to pick up that you are not exactly ecstatic about this,' she said, straight out. 'But I would remind you that it takes two to make a baby.' Her eyes met his, not letting them go. 'You were there as well. I thought we practised safe sex, but evidently not safe enough. The realisation that I was pregnant came as a shock to me, believe me— as much of a shock as it obviously has to you.'

She spoke calmly, but without backing down.

Without accusation or apology. Trying as best she could not to let the impact of seeing him again deflect her. She tried to stamp out her reaction. It would avail her nothing—only get in the way of what had to happen now. They needed to find some kind of agreement between them, for the sake of the baby she carried.

Why can't I just blank him? Oh, why can't I just be indifferent to him?

A mixture of resentment and futility filled her at how impossible that was.

She sought to infuse her voice with resolve. 'Whether we like it or not, Nikos, we have to deal with the situation.'

'Ah, yes, "the situation".' Nikos's voice echoed hers flatly. 'And just how do you we propose we do that?'

She searched his face, but there was nothing there. Nothing at all. She felt her heart sink again. But she couldn't give in—she had to keep going.

'Nikos,' she tried again, 'I'm really trying to make allowances for the fact that you are still coming to terms with me being pregnant. To keep remembering that I've had a lot longer than you to do so. But I can only assume you have *some* interest in the matter, or why bring me here to Athens? Why take me to see that obstetrician this morning if you don't intend to have anything to do with this baby?'

His expression did not change.

'That was simply to confirm that you are, indeed, pregnant.'

Alys stared. 'I'm past the first trimester, Nikos! This isn't something I'm imagining, believe me!'

She saw his mouth twist. 'But it is something you might have been lying about,' he said.

There was no emotion in his voice, nor in his face, and his eyes rested on her without expression. But there was a world of meaning in his words alone. Meaning that slammed into her as if a brick had hit her.

Two spots of colour flared in her cheeks. 'Well, now you know I'm not,' she got out tightly.

Disbelief filled her that he could think such a thing, but there was no opportunity to say more. Two waiters were sailing up to them, depositing their savoury first-course soufflés in front of them with a theatrical flourish. Alys could only be grateful for the interruption.

Is that really what he thinks of me? That I might have been lying to him?

Somewhere inside her she felt wounded—and it hurt. She fought for composure again, making herself pick up her spoon and start on the delicious-smelling soufflé.

Memory caught at her of how she'd relished eating the gourmet meal she'd shared with Nikos that one and only night with him. The night that had resulted in her being here now. The reason she was here. The *only* reason, she reminded herself bleakly. She felt the same wave of desolation sweep over her now as she had felt at the clinic.

I'm just a nuisance to him—he couldn't make it more obvious! He resents that I'm pregnant—wasn't even willing to believe it without proof! Well, if that's his attitude I can be likewise!

She put the spoon aside, her soufflé demolished. Then she lifted her head and looked across the table. Nikos still had that closed, remote look about him, and had already finished his soufflé. Alys took a breath. Directed her gaze right at him. This was not how she'd imagined it would be, but it was the way it was and she had no option but to deal with it. So she would be blunt—as blunt as he had been.

'You ask me what I want, Nikos. Well, I'll tell you. I'm in debt, and with a baby coming I have no way of paying it off.' She took a breath, knowing she must explain about the threat of foreclosure, of losing her home, the home she needed for her baby.

But she got no chance to tell him that.

'How much?' His voice cut across hers.

She swallowed. 'Twelve thousand pounds.' She'd added three months' extra repayments, to put her back in credit, to give herself a margin. 'And I… I need it right away.'

Her eyes were stuck on him, not daring to look away. Yet she could tell nothing about his reaction. She watched him, her anxiety mounting, hating it that she'd had to say it the way she had.

'And you would like me to settle that debt, would you not?' There was nothing in his voice—only expressionless enquiry.

Alys nodded. What else could she do?

'And so I will,' he answered.

His expression was still unreadable, but relief at what he'd said flooded through Alys. It was going to be all right! She wasn't going to lose her home! She and her baby were safe!

She opened her mouth to speak, splutter out her thanks, but he was holding a hand up, silencing her. His eyes rested on her face. Expressionless. Implacable.

'When,' Nikos said, 'we are married.'

Nikos heard himself speak, but it seemed to be coming from very far away. From somewhere he did not want to be. From somewhere he would be forced to be now, for all his life.

Just as my father was.

Savage emotion filled him—but what was the use of that?

'Married?'

The single word fell from Alys's lips.

The incredulity in her voice was genuine. Well, it might well be so. After all, it was probably something she'd never thought she could possibly achieve out of her fertility lottery win. A prize beyond her wildest dreams that made the paltry sum she wanted from him—only the beginning of her demands, that much was obvious!—nothing more than chickenfeed.

'Did you think it would be otherwise?' he returned.

She was still staring at him, and for some reason it annoyed him. Angered him.

'You cannot be serious?' he heard her say in hollow tones.

This time, as well as the incredulity he'd heard before, there was another note he had not. It annoyed him in the same way her staring at him annoyed him.

He levelled his gaze at her. 'No child of mine will be born a bastard,' he said.

He saw her flinch, saw colour flush her cheeks.

'Don't say that word! It's foul! And these days no one cares if parents are married!'

'*I* care,' he said. He knew there was steel in his voice. Adamantine steel. 'And because of that we will marry, Alys.'

He made his expression change. Made his voice lose the steeliness. Time for the next stage in this deal he had to bring to completion. And no deal he'd ever struck had been this critical—this essential for him to win.

'Don't look like that, Alys. There's no necessity for it. You will find being my wife very pleasant.' He changed his voice again. 'Indeed, exceptionally so.'

He reached inside his jacket, retrieved a small box.

'A small token, up-front,' he said, 'of all that you will enjoy as Kyria Drakis.'

His voice was dry...as dry as desert sand filled with the bones of the dead.

He flicked open the box.

Alys stared. Shock was still slicing through her and she was still not believing she could have heard him say what he had. To *marry* him?

Her gaze was glazed as she saw him flick open the lid of the satin box with long, powerful fingers. Fingers that were now sliding the open jewellery box towards her across the damask tablecloth.

'You should wear them now,' he was saying in that dry-as-a-desert voice, his eyes never leaving hers. 'They will suit your hairstyle tonight.'

She dropped her gaze. It seemed as heavy as lead, suddenly. Light from the candles on the tables caught the iridescence of pearl earrings, nestled against the silk of the box's lining.

Nikos was talking still. 'You see?' he was saying now, and his words seemed to be coming from a long way away. 'You see how very pleasant it will be for you to be Kyria Drakis? Jewellery such as this, designer dresses, couture gowns, chauffeur-driven limousines—a life of luxury awaits you, with everything you could dream of wanting all yours.'

There was something wrong with his voice. Something that cut like a knife to the very quick of her. She made no move to take the earrings, nor to push them back or touch them in any way. Yet she could feel, somewhere inside her head, words forming.

How beautiful they are! How exquisite! And they could be mine...

Her eyes were on him now, and she felt breathless suddenly. The smooth black of his dinner jacket sat perfectly across his broad shoulders and she looked at the tilt of his head, his dark, lidded eyes resting on her, the set of his sculpted mouth... The lethal combination of his looks and that seductive air of wealth, power and command. The leashed sensuality in the way he was looking at her now, holding her breathless gaze.

He could be mine...

Memory drowned her—of his skilled, effortless seduction of her that night she had gone to him. It could be hers again. *He* could be hers again.

Though her gaze never shifted from him, she could see in her peripheral vision the rest of the restaurant: its damask-covered tables, candlelight glinting on silverware and crystal glasses, and the jewellery of the expensive women dining here on gourmet food, drinking their vintage wine, living a life inconceivably distant from her own reality.

But it could be my reality... I could say goodbye to my old life. For ever.

The vision hovered like a tantalising dream within her reach.

Never again to be fearful of what bills and threats the day's post might bring…never to scrimp and save and search for budget items in the supermarket, snapping up food reduced for quick sale…never to walk to save the bus fare…never to shop for clothes in charity shops again.

To live instead a life not just of comfort and ease but wealth and luxury. And with Nikos.

Nikos! Nikos and me—like we were in London, but for always!

And why not? After all, what was there for her in England? Her mother was gone—she had nothing there to keep her! So why not think about what he had just said to her? Think about staying out here, in Greece. With him.

His wife. With his baby.

They would be making a family together—the kind of family she herself had never known…

For a moment so powerful it was unbearable, she let the image hang in her head. Then it crashed to the floor. The Nikos she had known in London, who had effortlessly seduced her into his arms, did not exist. Only this hard-faced, hostile man who couldn't be making it more obvious how unwelcome her pregnancy was.

Her eyes dropped to the earrings as she heard him telling her again how 'pleasant' life would be for her as his wife—as if that would be her only reason for marrying him.

He was still speaking but his face was shuttered, unreadable, his voice brisk and remote, business-like, and his completely unemotional, expression-less gaze was levelled at her. Alys felt her throat tighten, tension stiffen her as she listened to him. She could do nothing but listen, even as her dismay at what was coming from him mounted.

More than dismay.

Worse than dismay.

'The marriage will take place as soon as pos-sible,' he was saying, announcing it as if he was running through a prearranged list. 'However, be-fore that can be so, there is unavoidable paperwork to complete. You will need to send for your birth certificate—give me the details and I will see to it. I have already had an…an *appropriate*—' she heard a twist in his voice, an extra hardness '—pre-nuptial agreement drawn up for you to sign. The wedding ceremony itself will be civil only, privately conducted, with only ourselves and the requisite witnesses. Beforehand you will sign a non-disclosure agreement, again already drawn up by my lawyers, so that anything that passes between us will never be spoken of to the press or anyone else. Once we are married you will at all times conduct yourself in a manner befitting the wife of a Drakis. You will also sign a legal agree-ment giving me full custody of our child in the event of any divorce or of you giving me grounds for divorce such as adultery. The child will be a Greek citizen, and you will not be allowed to remove him or her from Greece for any reason without my express consent—all this will be legally binding. You will, for the duration of the marriage, be given an allowance adequate for your position as my wife, but you will not be permitted to run up any more debt, as seems to be your habit.'

She was hearing what he was saying—how could she not hear the ugly litany of conditions under which he would deign to marry her? And the even uglier assumptions that so obviously underlaid them. This was not about marriage—it was about control. Control of her, of her baby…

As if I'm an enemy—not the mother of his child!

It was repellent—repulsive.

She opened her mouth to speak, to stop what he was saying, to protest, but with every word that came from him her throat was tightening, as if a garotte was strangling her into forced silence, acquiescence.

When he reached the jibe about debt she flushed. She leant forward, desperate to speak. She had asked for that money because she wanted a roof over her head for her and for her baby—*his* baby! Not because she had been extravagant, or profligate! She wanted to explain, to justify herself—defend herself against what he was throwing at her.

Urgency filled her. She opened her mouth to speak, but he was not done yet.

'All of this, however,' he went on, in the same uninterruptible, blank-faced way, 'is entirely contingent upon the results of the test you will be having tomorrow morning, before we proceed any further with the wedding arrangements.'

Alys's expression changed, and her protest against what he'd announced—all the hostile conditions of how marriage to him would be and the ugly assumptions he was making about her—died on her lips.

'Test?' The single word fell from her. What he was saying to her was unreal.

Dismay was total within her. Mocking what she'd so stupidly, pathetically imagined only a handful of minutes ago.

Making a family together.

He was answering her question, but now his manner was not brisk and impersonal, as it had been when he was outlining the terms and conditions under which she, a lowly one-night stand who'd had the temerity to get herself pregnant by him, would become his wife. Because surely she could only possibly be interested in his money—why else would she have got in touch with him, come out here to Athens? And now, for the sake of the baby she so regrettably carried, she would have to become his wife—become Kyria Nikos Drakis, an honour she did not deserve—simply to legitimise a child he did not want and would never want *her* to be the mother of…

The garotte around her throat was still strangling her. But now, as he spoke on, she felt something like the blade of a knife sliding in under her ribcage. The final, deadly thrust of all he had dealt her.

'The test, Alys.' His voice was stark. 'The obstetrician this morning assured me it is perfectly safe, both for mother and baby—nothing more than a blood test for you, completely non-invasive, for which you are booked tomorrow morning.'

'I don't understand…' It was all she could get out, her voice hollow. She stared at him. What test could he mean?

And then Nikos's words were enlightening her.

'The test will show whether the child you are carrying, in your pregnancy that was confirmed this morning, is in fact mine.' He paused. His eyes were on her, yet completely empty. 'You do not imagine I will marry you without that assurance, do you, Alys?'

His words fell into the space between them. The space that was a chasm.

She was white—as white as bone. 'Who else's could it be, Nikos?'

She saw him shrug. A gesture of supreme indifference.

'How should I know or care into whose bed you fell before you fell into mine, or indeed after…?'

The garotte around her throat was tightening. 'How can you *think* that?'

His eyes rested on her, as empty as his voice.

'Alys, you were in my bed within hours of seeing me for the first time in your life. For all I know you make a habit of that every night—'

He got no further. The scrape of her chair silenced him. She propelled herself to her feet, incapable of enduring any more. Her whole body seemed to be shaking…her mind was in whiteout. Then she was walking towards the restaurant exit on legs that nearly buckled under her. A hysterical laugh wanted to burst from her—or something did. Something that was choking her, that she needed to expel.

He caught up with her before she could walk out, seizing her arm. 'Do *not* make a scene. I will not permit it!'

She could hear rage in his voice—as if, dear God, *he* had cause for anger.

His hand clamped around her arm, he led her out into the lobby, where he turned on her. 'This test *will* take place, Alys, protest all you want!' His hand dropped from her. 'Now, do you intend coming back to the table to finish your meal, or will you flounce off like a drama queen? There's still more to discuss. If you want me to pay your debts for you, you'll need to give me your bank account details and so forth. Of course that will have to await the outcome of the DNA test tomorrow, but—'

She stepped away from him, her face completely blank. Schooled into being so with the last threads of her self-control.

'I'd like to go back to the hotel, please.'

She heard her own voice speak, say all that she could cope with now. Inside her head a vortex had opened up and was sucking her down into it. Down, down, down.

For a moment Nikos just studied her, his own face still completely unreadable, as blank as hers was. Then he spoke, his voice clipped. 'Very well. I will make allowances for your condition. I can see you are in no state to continue this discussion or to finish your meal. I'll call for the car. But, Alys, do not imagine this is going to allow you to evade the test I require. Be ready for eleven tomorrow morning. The test will take place at the same clinic we attended this morning.'

She didn't bother to answer, or even to acknowledge what he'd said. Only turned and left the restaurant. With the vortex inside her swallowing her whole.

CHAPTER FIVE

NIKOS WALKED OUT onto the balcony of his apartment. The night was warm, but he felt cold. His expression was as dark as the night beyond. His mood darker.

So it was set in motion—what had to happen. What there was no possibility of avoiding.

Unless—

Unless the test tomorrow shows me another outcome.

Even as he made himself think it, emotion knifed in him. Yet he did not know from which direction it had struck.

There was only one rational emotion to feel, surely, if the test tomorrow told him he was not, after all, responsible for Alys's pregnancy.

Relief—that was all that he should feel. Relief that he would not be a father after all, that the baby was not his—

Yet why did the thought of it pierce like talons in his flesh?

He pushed it aside. It was not a negative result

that had to be dealt with, but its opposite. Just as his own father had had to.

He felt emotion churn within him, demanding admittance, but he would not allow it. Clenching his hands instead, thrusting them deep into his pockets, he stood, legs apart, gazing blindly out over the city of his birth. A birth his father had never wanted...had deplored all his life and still did—with every barbed reproach, every challenge designed to enforce the fact that he had to prove, endlessly, that he was worthy of being a Drakis. Yet he was perpetually resented for being one. For having been forced upon his father.

He could hear his father's bitterly familiar refrain—one he'd grown up with.

"'There will be no Drakis bastards!' That's what my own father held over me! Forcing me to marry! Ruining my life for me!'

It mocked him now, thinking of the very word he'd spoken that evening over dinner. More than mocked him. The emotion he would not allow admittance to pressed again. He thrust it back. There was no place for it. No place for anything other than doing what he had already done, doing what he must yet do.

He stared out over the city, brilliant with lights, at the Parthenon on the Acropolis, floodlit to the stars above, his hands numbed in their clenched fists.

Feeling nothing.

The safest thing to feel.

It was an admonition he continued to level at himself the next morning as, steely-faced, he walked into the hotel he'd booked Alys into. Alys…the woman who had rocked his senses so disastrously in the impulsive, reckless passion of a single night, who now might or might not be carrying his child. And if she were, then he would do the only thing that must be done.

But he found her not waiting for him, ready to be collected, as she'd been yesterday. He strode, annoyed, to the desk, to have her telephoned. Only to hear, in apologetic tones, that Miss Fairford was no longer at the hotel.

That she'd checked out two hours earlier.

After asking for the quickest way to the airport.

Alys stood in the security queue, willing it to move faster, her tension sky-high. She would not feel safe until she was through Departures and in her seat on the plane—bought at the airport, as cheaply as she could. Which wasn't cheap at all in her precariously overstretched budget.

She wanted to give a hysterical laugh. She had come here hoping above all that the crushing debt hanging over her, jeopardising her and her precious baby's future, might be lifted from her—only for now to be even deeper in debt, to the tune of the price of a flight back to London.

And when I get there I'll have to face what I've

desperately tried to avoid. Losing my house, my home, my baby's home...

Because her one hope to save it had gone, and now she must sell it in time to meet the arrears payment deadline or lose it to foreclosure.

But she dared not think of that—not yet, not now. Dared not give vent to any emotion at all— not a single one. Lest they rip her to pieces.

She could feel them twisting like fanged snakes inside her, tightening and tugging and knotting, as they had been all night. She'd lain there sleepless, tormented, desperate for morning so that she could do what she was doing now.

Fleeing from the nightmare she had walked into.

Because *anything*—even losing her home—was better than what she now knew Nikos had planned for her.

A grotesque mockery of a marriage! With him despising me even as he forces himself to marry me! Wishing to God he didn't have to! Thinking I've trapped him! Hating me for it!

But she must not let herself play and replay, over and over again, as she had all through her hideous, sleepless night, what he had said to her, how he had shown what he thought of her.

All she must do now was urge the queue forward, try to push it on with her exhausted mind, one hand clenching the handle of her carry-on suitcase, the other clutching, with aching fingers, her precious passport and boarding pass.

And now she was nearly there, inching her way forward towards Departures, with only a few people left ahead of her now. She focussed on them, trying to distract herself from the seething emotions writhing within her. It wasn't good to be so upset and agitated...it wasn't good for her baby...

I've got to keep calm—I've got to!

But it was impossible. Deep within she felt her insides clutch, her throat constrict. Her face puckered. Her eyes stung like acid.

She blinked rapidly, hating it that she was so close to the edge, so near to plunging over...

The four people ahead of her were now only three, now only two...decreasing with glacial slowness. Her hand was numb with the tightness of her grip on her ready-opened passport. Only one more person in front of her now—

'Alys.'

The voice behind her, the sound of her name, cut through the airport's hubbub.

She spun round, stomach plunging.

Nikos.

Striding towards her, black fury in his face.

Oh, no. No, no...

Terror seized her like a wolf savaging her throat. Paralysing her.

'Alys.'

Her name came again. His voice was more demanding now. Harder. Harsher. Angrier.

Her elbow was seized, immobilising her.

'What the *hell* are you playing at?'

Nikos was looming over her, so much taller than she was, overpowering her with his presence.

Words broke from her. Protest. Vehement and vital.

'Let me go! *Let me go!* I'm going home! Back to England!'

His face darkened. '*What?* Don't be absurd!'

She shook herself free, wrenching back from him. With a fragment of her mind she was aware that the queue was moving forward again. It would be her turn next. And she *must* get through.

But Nikos had seized her elbow again, his grip like iron, his face black with fury.

'You're going nowhere! Do you understand me? You're coming back! Do you hear me? I won't have this!'

She could feel him pulling her away, out of the queue, could see the rage in his face, his eyes.

She broke.

Broke as if she had been snapped in half.

She was shouting back at him. Face contorting. Fury fuelled to flashover. 'No, *I* won't have it, Nikos! *I* won't! I won't have anything to do with you! I wish to God I'd never come here!'

Her voice was rising dangerously, desperately. Emotion was storming through her—uncontrollable, unstoppable. She felt his grip tighten on her, and with a cry of rage she flung it off.

'Don't touch me! Don't come near me! Get away from me!'

People were turning, looking at them, stepping back. But she didn't care—she didn't care about anything. She was way past that.

Now he was trying to catch at her hand, but she knocked him away, feeling her passport and boarding pass become dislodged from her grip as she did so. With a cry of distress she stooped down to pick them up, abandoning her grip on her carry-on. She had to have them. She couldn't get into Departures without them. And she had to get through, had to get away from this vile, foul man...

Her cry of distress came again. Higher now. More frantic. She was scrabbling on the ground, desperate to seize up her passport, her boarding pass. But she couldn't hold them, her fingers were clawing uselessly, hands flailing, and she couldn't see. She could only cry out again, yelling at him to get away from her, her voice rising in desperate urgency.

'Alys!'

There was something different in his voice now. It was not demanding any more, but alarmed. And now he was stooping down beside her, retrieving the scattered passport and boarding pass, straightening, taking her up with him, grabbing hold of her pull-along, trying to place an arm around her waist, to draw her away.

Away from the sanctuary she was trying to

reach in Departures, where she would be safe from him. Out of the queue she mustn't lose her place in.

'Let me go!' Her voice was high and thin, and she was trying to snatch back her passport and boarding pass, pummelling frantically at his chest, anywhere she could reach, almost insane with desperation. 'I'm not going back with you. You can't make me! You can take your bloody paternity tests and marriage proposals and you can *choke* on them! I wouldn't marry you if you crawled on your belly to me!'

Her rising voice was shaking like a leaf in a storm, ripped from her throat, which was constricting so much that she couldn't breathe, couldn't talk, couldn't do anything at all but flail at him with her hands.

'So just get off me! Do you hear me? Get off me and go to hell, Nikos Drakis. And take your stinking money with you! You're the last man on God's earth I'd want for my baby's father!'

The words were spewing from her as her fists thumped uselessly against him. Because he would not let her go. And now there were people running up to her, footsteps and agitated voices, all speaking in Greek. Still her hands were pummelling at him, but he would not leave her—would not do anything except give orders in that stentorian voice of his, though it was speaking in Greek now.

She felt an arm come around her waist, but it wasn't his because he was stepping away from her, and then a woman's voice was speaking to her, saying words that she could not understand, and she was being drawn away, gently but insistently, across the concourse into a room that opened off it. She was led to a couch of some kind, pressed down upon it, and now she wasn't yelling any longer, only shaking…

And then someone else was looming over her. A man in a white coat, with a stethoscope around his neck, and he was talking to her. This time she heard—understood—what he was saying to her, speaking in accented English.

'I am the airport doctor—for emergencies, you understand—and you are here in the medical room. And you must be calm, because this agitation is not good for you—nor for your baby. So please, take slower breaths. You are hyperventilating and your pulse is racing, and this is not good. You are safe here…quite safe.' He was chafing her hand gently, looking down at her reassuringly. 'You must sit here quietly, for a little while, and my nurse is making you a cup of tea, and that will help to calm you too.'

He went on talking quietly to her, encouraging her to slow her breathing, and she could feel it easing, feel her hectic heart rate slowing. The nurse brought a mug of tea over, a tisane, and Alys took it numbly, sipping it slowly as the doctor directed. Little by little she felt the storm of emotion subside within her, her shaking cease, her throat untighten as she drank her tea.

When she had finished it, the doctor spoke again, his voice still calm and reassuring.

'And now you need to rest for a little while. Rest completely.'

He was lifting her legs onto the couch, and she was tilted back, sinking against its contours into the cushions behind her. He was taking the empty mug from her and her eyelids were fluttering. They were heavy, and she did not want to see the world…she wanted to shut it away.

Her breathing slowed and sleep came, blessed sleep, after her endless sleepless night, the tumult of her emotions, the desperate race to the airport, the hideous storm of adrenaline that had rushed over her just now. It all drained away into stricken exhaustion, and she was finally released from a consciousness she could no longer bear.

Nikos sat in the plastic armchair in the medical room Alys had been taken to by the female security guard who had come running up as she had stormed and flailed at him. He sat motionless, watching her lie so still and pale on the couch, her chest rising and falling in exhausted sleep.

The doctor had gone, after instructing a nurse to fetch him again as needed, and the nurse had covered Alys with a light blanket before busying herself with paperwork at the desk nearby.

Nikos's eyes rested on Alys. She looked as if a gust of wind might blow her away. He went on watching her, still in shock from what had just happened. Her fury, her incandescent rage at him—her outrage!—had been so real, so blazing...

It had shaken him to the core.

He sat completely still, but behind his expressionless face his mind was racing.

Is that truly how she feels?

But how could he doubt it? He'd been on the receiving end of it—seen it in her eyes, in her face, heard it in her voice. Total and absolute meltdown...

A sombre furrow creased his brow. There had been more than anger in the words she'd hurled at him, in the fists pummelling at his chest. She had seemed almost...distraught—as if everything had become too much for her to bear. Her face had contorted not just with fury, but with distress—as if a moment longer and she'd have been in uncontrollable floods of tears...

As if I'd pushed her beyond her limits, wounded her, hurt her...

The thought, unwelcome, and unwanted, hung in his head. He did not want to credit it...to believe it. He fought against it. He *knew* what she was! A woman he'd rashly fallen into bed with, after succumbing to the overpowering desire of a moment, who now was intent on doing to him what his own mother had done to his father.

His expression darkened.

What Miriam intended to do to me—to make use of the Drakis millions, shamelessly exploit my devotion to her.

His mouth set. Hadn't Alys openly admitted last night that she had debts? And was that not the reason she'd come out here? Because she wanted him to pay them off for her?

But then why bolt this morning? Why unleash her fury on me when I told her she could have all the luxuries of being my wife?

Grimly, he realised he knew the answer to that.

It was when I said I would insist on a paternity test—that was what sent her flying!

He felt his jaw tighten, aching with the tension that was racking his body, as he tried to make sense of what he could not make any sense of at all.

Had it been his demand for a paternity test before they married that had made her flee, lest the truth exploded all her hopes of getting any money at all from him?

But what she hurled at me was not that she knew she could not get what she wanted from me! She threw back in my face everything I'm prepared to do for her! As if it were poison to her! As if I am poison to her—

His hands clenched on his knees, his gaze searching her face. His eyes rested on her as if seeing her for the first time.

And into his head came a memory. A memory

that had nothing to do with the jolt of lightning-force electricity that had arced between them when he'd first seen her across that crowded cocktail lounge all those months ago in London. Nothing to do with the way his eyes had fastened on her last night as she'd approached the restaurant table wearing that dress that had made her look so stunningly beautiful that every male head in the place had turned instinctively towards her.

No, this was a different memory.

The way she looked the morning I left her lying in my bed—her face bare of make-up, her hair flowing across the pillow—so very lovely that I wanted to reach down and kiss her softly, possessively, make her mine again, knowing I must not... The regret I felt as I left her...

His gaze flickered over her again now, taking in something more than her fragile stricken beauty. Taking in, for the first time, the way her hand was resting over the blanket draped across her, her fingers gently cupping her abdomen. As if shielding the baby she carried invisibly within.

He felt emotions clench inside him. Emotions he dared not confront or admit to. Questions flickered inside his head as he gazed at her.

What do I do now? What should I do? I thought I had her sussed. I thought it was obvious what had happened to me—I'd been caught in the same benighted honeytrap that was sprung on my father! I thought that meant I knew exactly what I had to do.

But now only one thing was certain.

He took a deep and silent breath, feeling at last some of the unanswerable conflicts in his mind distil into resolution. He did not know the truth about her—could not know...not yet—but one thing he did know with searing certainty. She must not flee him again.

So I have to find another way forward. I have to keep her here. But how? And where?

Not in Athens—somewhere quiet and remote and private.

His mind raced, searching for a solution that would work.

And where it came from he did not know, but suddenly it was there in his head. That fragment of his mentioning on that long-ago evening he'd spent with her in London his family villa in the Aegean, Villa Drakis.

His eyes lit. Yes, he would take her there! It was quiet, remote and private—just what he needed. Relief filled him at how perfect a solution it would provide. It was hardly used any more—he hadn't been for years, and his father had never cared for it. It stood there empty but for the maintenance staff. Ideal for his purpose.

He felt some of his tension subside. Now all he had to do, when she awoke, was persuade Alys to agree.

And once they were there...

His face grew sombre, and there was a darker look in his eyes now.

Then I find another way to achieve what I need to.

Alys was stirring. Light was pressing on her eyelids, pushing her back into the world. As her eyes flickered open she saw Nikos sitting opposite her. She opened her mouth to gasp in protest, but no sound came out. Then the nurse was standing up, coming across to her, picking up her hand to take her pulse, releasing it with a smile.

'Much slower,' she announced reassuringly.

Alys sat up, her body heavy and lethargic. She didn't want Nikos Drakis there. Didn't want him anywhere near her ever again.

But he was leaning forward, speaking to her. 'Alys, please...we have to talk.'

She made herself look at him. There was something different about him. He was less arrogant. Less hard... And his tone of voice wasn't the way it had been when he'd accosted her in the Departures queue, the way it had been since the moment she'd arrived here in Athens.

Alys frowned. He sounded almost diffident. Her frown deepened. Nikos Drakis didn't *do* diffident. He did orders and high-handed diktats and contemptuous insults.

And I'm done with all of those!

She shook her head. 'No, we don't have to talk

at all. All I have to do is get my flight—or the next one, I don't care which—and go home.'

He reached out a hand towards her, as if to stay her. 'Don't go,' he said. Then he let his hand drop and turned to the nurse, speaking in English to her. 'Will you allow us a few minutes, if you please?'

The nurse hesitated, glancing at Alys, but when she made no objection, conceded, 'Very well—but there must be no more agitation.'

Nikos nodded, giving her his assurance. And as the nurse left, he turned back to Alys. There was something else different about him now that she'd not seen before. Hesitation.

'Alys…' His eyes rested on her and there was something different about them too, she realised. 'Please hear me out.'

His tone was guarded, and she could see he was watching for her reaction. She eyed him warily. She might as well let him get on with whatever he was going to say, and then she would pick up her bag and get the hell out of here…find a flight she could get on and get Nikos Drakis out of her life for good—the way he had to be now that she knew just what he thought of her.

She felt something bitter twist inside her, tightening her expression as she looked at him, her face stony. He seemed to pause, to look for what he wanted to say, which she did not wish to hear anyway, and then he spoke.

'I am sorry that you were so upset,' he began. 'I… I want to make amends.'

Amends? Her mouth twisted in derision, the word mocking her.

'I don't want it to be like this between us,' Nikos said.

His eyes held hers. Hers flashed angrily. 'How the hell else can it be?' she demanded, derision still in the twist of her mouth. 'After what you've said to me?'

'Alys, I—'

Emotion started to knife in her again, and she would not let him finish. 'You don't even think the baby is yours! You want me to have some slut-shaming paternity test to rule out all the other men I must obviously have slept with as well as you!'

His mouth set. 'That was crass of me,' he answered. 'And I apologise.'

Alys looked at him, the stab of emotion dying away as swiftly as it had arisen. She had no energy for any more emotion. And her chest had tightened again, though she did not want it to. And here he was, telling her he was apologising.

She felt her throat constrict and wondered why. It was as if tears were threatening. But why should that be? He had no power to *hurt* her—only people who meant something to her could hurt her—and what did Nikos Drakis mean to her? Nothing—less than nothing!

Acid welled in her mouth, souring it, and she

heard him speak again in that strange, different voice he was using. The voice that went with the frowning, troubled look on his face, the tension in his brow, his stark cheekbones.

'Alys, hear me out. I haven't handled this well. You're upset, and I understand that, but I want things to be different.'

She saw him draw breath, and then he continued, his eyes never leaving her face, though she kept herself expressionless—because she could not, *would* not, do anything more.

'So what I propose is this. That we leave Athens and go somewhere where there is peace and quiet and rest for you.' He paused. 'You may recall I mentioned that evening we spent together in London that my family has a villa on one of the Aegean islands. It is beautiful, and very peaceful, and I think it will do you good. We will stay for as long as it takes. It will help you…adjust. It will help us both do so.'

His eyes were meeting hers, but what was in them Alys didn't know. All she knew was what was in herself.

'You want me,' she said slowly, incredulously, 'to let you take me to some island—I have no idea where—and lock me away in a villa…? You really think I'm going to agree to that? To go with you? To *trust* you?'

'*No*—I give you my word. You may leave at any time, Alys. But I hope,' he said, his eyes never leaving hers, 'that you will not wish to leave—that you find peace there…and a respite that is good for you, for your baby.'

He paused, and something shifted in his eyes. Was it a veiling or a hesitation? She didn't know—knew only that she was hearing him speak and that his words were holding her as if she were in a bubble, suspended in the air.

'Yesterday, Alys…'

He was speaking again, and it seemed those dark, deep eyes that had so entranced her so long ago were probing hers, as if seeking answers she did not want to give.

'Yesterday you mentioned you had debts.' His expression changed minutely. 'Last night I said they must wait, but…' He took another breath, his gaze intent. 'Allow me to pay them right now. To put your mind at rest. To show my…my good faith.'

She stared at him. 'Why?' she said. Her voice was thin. Tiredness was dragging her down. And confusion too.

Nikos Drakis…talking to me of 'good faith'?

'I have said—to show my good faith,' he repeated. 'And in return you'll agree to come to my villa, as I have asked of you.'

He slid his phone out of his jacket pocket. 'Tell me what your bank details are and I will have the sum of twelve thousand pounds—that's what you said last night?—transferred right now.'

He was holding her eyes, but she could not

hold his in return. She shut her eyes against him. Thoughts, hectic and heavy, clattered against the edges of her mind, demanding entry. She was too tired to stop them.

He says he'll pay it straight away! Right now! Twelve thousand pounds! It's what you're desperate for! Just take it!

Her eyes screwed tighter. She would sooner eat broken glass than take his money now!

Then you're a fool! You're thinking of yourself, of your own pride! He's the father of your child, however foul his accusations that he might not be! Twelve thousand pounds is chickenfeed to him! But to you it's the lifeline you desperately need.

Fear stabbed at her. She knew just what would happen if she failed to find that money—she would lose her home. The home she needed for her baby.

'Alys…'

Nikos's voice was in her ears again, making her open her eyes, look at him.

'Give me your bank account details so I can make the transfer. Right now.'

There was insistence in his voice, but she felt herself looking around, wondering belatedly what had happened to her luggage. Her carry-on was propped in the corner, and on top of it was her handbag.

Nikos saw her looking and reached for it, handing it to her. Hardly knowing what she was doing, she opened it with nerveless, fumbling fingers. The fatal letter threatening foreclosure lay at the bottom of her bag, but she did not take it out, only clumsily unfolded it enough to make out the account details and the sort code, given by the mortgage company, into which she must make the payment of her arrears. Chest tight, she read it out to Nikos, and he keyed it into his phone.

It was done in moments, and he slid the phone away, looking back at her. 'It's gone through,' he said.

And now there was yet another note in his voice she could not recognise, and something in his eyes that shifted minutely and then was gone. But she was still trying to take in the reality of what had just happened—that in a few swift keystrokes he'd lifted the terrifying threat hanging over her head.

He got to his feet. 'I'm going to arrange our transport to the island. Sit quietly till I return. I'll call the nurse back.'

She watched him walk out of the medical room and heard him say something in Greek—to the nurse, presumably, who promptly came back in, coming up to Alys and asking how she was, bringing her a glass of water to drink.

Numbly, she complied, then sat back, eyes closed. Wanting to feel relief that the threat that had been hanging over her for so long had vanished. Yet feeling nothing. Knowing, somewhere in the exhausted recesses of her mind, that 'nothing' was all she could cope with right now.

As to what would come next—she could not even go there…

CHAPTER SIX

THE PRIVATE AIRCRAFT that he'd chartered at short notice from Athens was touching down on the short island runway, taxiing towards the private section of the small airport. A handful of minutes later Nikos was vaulting down the extended steps, slowly followed by Alys, who was looking about her, saying nothing. She'd barely spoken on the flight, seeming to close in on herself. He'd let her be, making no demands on her.

He picked up Alys's carry-on case and guided her towards an SUV waiting nearby, summoned there by his phone call from Athens to Spiros, who looked after the Villa Drakis.

He opened the front passenger door before loading her case into the boot. She'd got in, and he did too, to see keys waiting in the ignition for him.

He gunned the engine. 'It's about a forty-minute drive to the villa,' he said, heading out across the tarmac to the perimeter gate.

Alys made no answer to his remark, and Nikos was glad of her silence. It gave him space for his own thoughts. He'd got her here—now he had to plan what happened next.

One goal was paramount.

I've got to stop her hostility towards me. Defuse it. I need her to co-operate—to want to co-operate.

But he could afford to make no more mistakes.

At least he'd succeeded in persuading her to come here with him.

Yes, by paying off her debts! Exactly what she wanted of you!

He felt a pull of acid cynicism at how readily she'd let him do so, then sought to quell it. He'd made the offer to pay, said it was to show his good faith.

And maybe that's what I have to keep on doing. Showing good faith.

His glance went to her. She'd closed her eyes, resting her head back. Her face was in repose, but strain was still visible in it…the marks of that raging meltdown at the airport. It had shaken his conviction that he knew exactly why she had come out to Greece at his invitation, exactly what her goal was.

But then she should have bitten my hand off for the chance to marry me! Not just wanted a paltry few thousand to pay off her debts!

It didn't make sense. *She* didn't make sense.

His eyes went back to the road ahead. He was taking the coastal route that hugged the rocky contours of the island, heading to the northern promontory on which Villa Drakis sat in remote seclusion—ideal for a member of the Greek plutocracy who did not wish to be bothered by tourists or the hoi polloi.

From time to time his glance went to her, and thoughts threaded in and out of his consciousness as he drove, glad that he could look at her without her being conscious of it. It seemed almost impossible to believe that she was here, sitting beside him, just because of one searing night together...

Why did it happen, that night with her? What was it about her that made me unable to resist her?

Memory took him back to seeing her at the entrance to that cocktail lounge, to his eyes fastening on her as if it had been impossible to do otherwise.

Her wild and wanton hair, her huge eyes, lush mouth, fantastic figure had been fully on display to him—the whole irresistible package.

But it wasn't that alone that drew me to her. Made me reach for her...

Made him act so out of character that he'd helped himself to her that very night, throwing caution to the winds, acting on an impulse so strong he had not denied it to himself. Denied *her* to himself...

And when I took her in my arms and she melted into me she was not as I thought she would be, expected her to be! Ardent, oh, yes, but not...

Not experienced.

Not a virgin, true, but there had been a shyness to her as he laid bare her naked loveliness, her pale cheeks colouring as he'd explored the intimacies of her body with leisurely caresses…

He shifted in his driver's seat, exerting torque on the steering wheel as the road snaked around a narrowing bend. He glanced at her again as he came out of the bend, flickering over her.

It hadn't been wise to remember their night together in such detail. And nor was it wise, now, to remember that flight across the Atlantic when he'd made the decision to have more than one single night with her—to seek her out.

And now she is here, beside me, heading to the villa with me. Where I will have her all to myself…

He gave a shake of his head. He was bringing her here only to stop her bolting back to England before he had the answers he *had* to have.

His glance went to her yet again, his eyes caressing the delicate contours of her soft cheeks, the tender swell of her lips, the smoky lashes dark against her pale skin…

How very lovely she was.

He felt temptation lick at him, move within him. Making him think thoughts that he should resist.

Wasn't the situation complicated enough, as it was?

And yet…

One night with her was not enough after all—I wanted more. And now—

Now she was here with him, at his side, heading to his villa. And while she was there…

His thoughts moved, taking form and shape. Making sense...

In my arms she will not oppose me...will not seek to leave me...

The thought hovered, tantalising and so tempting...

And after all, if the baby is indeed mine, then...

Then there could be only one outcome. Just as he had spelled out to her last night.

And this time she would not *want* to turn him down.

Alys sat with her eyes closed as the SUV headed forward. Had she been mad, letting Nikos bring her to some island she'd never heard of, to his private villa there? He'd said she would be free to leave whenever she wanted. That she had his word. Was his word worth anything? She didn't know. She didn't know anything about him.

Except that he thinks I'd be fine with foisting another man's baby on him and ecstatic at the thought of having all his stinking money to spend as his wife.

Anger, as familiar as it was bitter, twisted inside her. But what did she care what he thought of her?

What I care about is that he's paid off my mortgage arrears so I won't lose my home.

It would be a penny-pinching life—just as her own mother had experienced—but she would manage. As for Nikos…he could go to hell. She would take not a penny from him in maintenance.

To think she had hoped that his financial support would enable her to dedicate herself to her baby, as her own mother had not been able to.

But better that than what Nikos offered me! A toxic marriage, with him hating that he has to endure it.

No, even if she was doomed to repeat exactly the kind of life her own mother had had, it would still be better than the one Nikos wanted to impose on her.

The sound of Nikos saying her name roused her from her embittered thoughts.

'Alys—we've arrived.'

She opened her eyes. They had pulled up on a gravelled forecourt, with garaging to one side. In front was the wall of a white building that had only narrow windows in it, and a central door which was now opening. A figure was emerging, coming up to Nikos as he got out of the car, addressing him in Greek.

Nikos lifted a hand in greeting, then came around to Alys's door to open it for her. She climbed out, not taking the hand Nikos was holding out to her.

'Alys, this is Spiros, who looks after everything here,' Nikos announced.

She nodded, and got an effusive smile in return

as the man went around to the boot to extract her small suitcase.

She let Nikos usher her forward, carefully keeping her distance from him. She could feel her heart beating in her chest, which felt tight as a drum. As she stepped through the doorway she found herself on a small landing, from which a flight of wide stone stairs led down to a circular, atrium-style hall, off which were set doors at intervals.

She headed down the stairs, holding the banister as the steps curved round. At the foot, a maid was holding open a door, smiling in a welcoming fashion. Spiros nipped past her, carrying her suitcase. Alys followed him into a room.

Her gaze swept around. It was a beautifully appointed bedroom, in creams and blues, with louvred blinds on the floor-to-ceiling windows, creating a cool shade emphasised by the air con.

The maid was busy starting to unpack, but Alys stayed her. 'It's fine—I'll do it.'

The maid smiled and left her to it, closing the bedroom door behind her. Still feeling numb, all emotions tamped down, Alys headed into the en suite bathroom. It was as beautifully appointed as the bedroom, with a huge walk-in shower with both rainfall and jetted shower heads, a marble-topped vanity unit inset with a massive basin, with a whole array of expensive-looking toiletries lined up beside it and piles of fluffy white towels on the shelving.

The room was making her feel weary, and grimy, longing to freshen up. Hardly realising what she was doing, she started to strip off. Moments later she was standing under the pounding shower, letting the pummelling water wash all thought from her.

Nikos walked into the master bedroom, sliding back the capacious fitted wardrobe in the dressing area, looking for something more comfortable than the business suit he was wearing. There was probably something left here from whenever he'd last visited. When *had* he last visited? he wondered. He tried to think and failed. Years, definitely. But then, of course, he got so little time off to go anywhere that wasn't work-related.

He sifted through some assorted beachwear and casualwear, chucking a selection on the bed before shrugging out of his jacket, extracting his phone as he did so. He'd made use of his time on the flight over by contacting his PA, updating her on a few urgent matters, then coolly instructing her to cancel all his appointments—home and abroad—indefinitely.

His father would kick off, but he didn't care. He had a far more important matter to attend to, and he didn't want work calls distracting him.

His mouth thinned. If his father was that fussed, he could deal with them himself, for once.

He tossed his phone into the top drawer of his bedside table. From now on it would not be a priority.

Alys stepped out of the shower, wrapping herself in a huge fleecy bath sheet, twisting her newly washed hair into a towel turban, padding back into the bedroom on bare feet. She felt...*revived*. She sank down on the soft bed, lying back. The heat from the shower and the dim light in the shaded room, together with the cumulative sleep debt from her sleepless night, all made her feel drowsy. She felt her eyelids grow heavy...

It was a soft knock on the door that roused her. One of the maids was there, telling her in accented English that Kyrios Drakis awaited her on the terrace, if she cared to join him.

Alys stood up, murmuring her thanks, and the maid disappeared again, leaving Alys to extract fresh undies from her suitcase and try and decide what to wear. She had packed for Athens—not luxury villas in the Aegean.

In the end she selected a denim skirt and a loose white top, slipping her bare feet into the flats she'd worn to the airport. Her thoughts flickered. Had Nikos not intercepted her before she'd got to Departures she'd be back in England now.

Instead...

She took a breath. Yes, well, she was here now. To what purpose she had no idea. Nor did she care.

You and me, my darling baby—we're all that matters. No one else.

Least of all Nikos. He could go to hell and stay there.

Face set, she left the bedroom and walked across the central atrium. Double doors had been flung open, opposite the foot of the stairs, and she made for them. Deep gold light filled the room beyond— a lavishly appointed lounge set with white sofas and floor rugs—and she stepped inside.

Immediately she made for the bifold doors drawn aside almost the entire length of the external wall. It was impossible to do otherwise. She stepped out onto a broad terrace that opened directly off the lounge. The rich gold light that had drawn her was drenching the world. It was the sun, lowering to the right of her, bathing the vista in its rays.

And such a vista it was—a sweeping semicircle of azure sea extending around a low promontory that projected out beyond the terraced gardens that tumbled down to beaches on either side. She could do nothing but stare, drinking in the breathtaking panorama.

'We get both sunrise and sunset here. Right now, it's sunset…'

Nikos's voice to her left made her turn. He was strolling towards her from further along the terrace. Against her will, Alys felt her breath catch. He was bathed in the golden light from the lowering sun, which was turning his skin to bronze, and his dark hair glinted with gold, etching his features. He was no longer in the sombre business suit that made him look so remote, so austere—so forbidding. He'd changed into buff-coloured chinos and a pale blue cotton shirt open at the collar, cuffs turned back, showing sinewed forearms dusted with gold.

He looked incredible…

She swallowed, unable to tear her eyes away, feeling her pulse surge. Helpless to stop it.

'Pretty good, isn't it? The sunset…'

He was speaking again, and Alys made herself breathe, forcing back control. She was not here to be struck breathless by the sight of Nikos Drakis. That was no part of the reason she was here. *None.* Never again…

She swallowed. 'Yes,' she said, because she had to say something.

He smiled. 'I'd forgotten how spectacular the view is from here,' he said. His eyes met hers. 'This is a good place, Alys. I'm glad you've come.'

There was something different in his voice. Something that had not been there before. Something she did not want to hear. Something that she wanted to block.

She made no reply, and he spoke again.

'Let me get you something to drink. What would

you like?' He gestured to a drinks trolley nearby. 'There's a variety of juices to choose from.' He reeled them off for her.

'Pomegranate, please,' Alys said. Her voice was clipped, doggedly neutral.

She watched him cross to the trolley, half fill a tumbler with ice, then top it up with dark red juice. He handed it to her, poured a beer for himself and raised his glass.

'*Yammas,*' he said.

Memory stung her. That was what he'd said in London, when they'd shared cocktails together. Before sharing so much more…

She dragged her eyes away, walking towards the stone balustrade at the edge of the terrace and looking over at the gardens plunging down the steep drop in a series of terraced beds, verdant with glossy-leaved greenery and festooned with swathes of vivid bougainvillea. She lifted her gaze to the setting sun, now turning to bronze, pooling on the horizon with the sea that was also turned to bronze as the two touched together. Thoughts jumbled in her head—memories that she didn't want, that had no place any more. She banished them ruthlessly, closing in on herself again.

She became aware that Nikos had also come up to the balustrade, positioning himself a little way away from her. But he said nothing, only stood as she was standing, watching the sun set over the encircling sea. In the bushes, lush with bougainvillea, heavy with the scent of jasmine as the evening came on, the ceaseless chorus of the cicadas seemed to intensify.

It was easy to stand there, even with Nikos so close, and pay attention to the incredible display Nature was putting on before her eyes as, imperceptibly, the sun slowly pooled into the waiting water, spreading out its last crimson glow before, almost with a sigh, it was swallowed up.

Dusk gathered, and she could no longer see the colour of the flowers. She saw only the dim white of the jasmine, and caught its heady night scent in her nostrils.

She saw Nikos lever himself away from the balustrade, drain his beer. Behind them, she was aware of maids turning on lights in the lounge, placing candles and a freestanding lamp on a table further along the terrace—set, Alys realised, for dinner.

Nikos put his empty glass down on the drinks trolley. 'Shall we?' he asked, indicating the table.

She didn't answer, only walked towards it. Still closed in on herself, knowing it was the only way she could cope right now.

The warm night air embraced her like a soft shawl as Nikos pulled a chair out for her, and she sat herself down as he took the one opposite. Spiros emerged onto the terrace, with a young man-servant behind him carrying a large and laden tray.

She heard Nikos exchange what she assumed

were pleasantries with the young man as he deposited a platter of *mezze* between them, while Spiros placed a bottle of opened wine beside Nikos. He murmured his thanks and dismissed them.

He looked across at Alys. 'I hope this is to your liking…dining al fresco?' he enquired solicitously.

Alys nodded. A sense of unreality was unfolding over her. Last night Nikos had treated her as if she were a promiscuous, gold-digging tramp. And now…

Now it's as if I'm a welcome guest—to be treated with courtesy and solicitude.

The difference was bizarre. And tasted bitter in her throat.

Wariness filled her.

He was lifting up the wine bottle, speaking again. 'Will you have any wine at all, Alys?' Again, as before, there was nothing but courteous enquiry in his voice.

She shook her head, reaching for the jug of iced water on the table to top up her pomegranate juice. Then Nikos was indicating the platter of *mezze*, telling her what each delicacy was, placing a selection on her plate.

She began to eat, making herself not look at Nikos, though she was aware of him all the time, because she almost could not stop herself. She was aware of how he helped himself to more from the platter, how he lifted his wine glass to wash it down, how the soft light from the table lamp cast a glow over him, like *chiaroscuro* across his planed features, throwing them into relief.

Tormentingly aware.

He made light conversation. Nothing that demanded any reply from her. Telling her about the villa, that there was a swimming pool lower down, and a beach on either side, walks to the tip of the promontory beyond. That the larger beach to the left-hand side had a quay and a small boathouse, containing a dinghy and a motorboat.

She listened because there was nothing else to do. Her sense of unreality was paramount. She was actually here, in this luxurious villa, on this sea-girt island in the Aegean, dining with a man she had fled from only this morning...

Wariness flickered in her again.

Yes, with a few careless keystrokes he had lifted from her the crushing burden that had been hanging over her head, that she had been so desperate to dispel, and yet it had happened only because she had agreed to come here with him.

But why?

Was it just to renew that nightmare demand he'd made of her about the paternity test? The demand that had shown her just what he thought of her? But her answer would be the same—total refusal. How could it be otherwise?

She gave up trying to think, simply folded her numbed wariness around her, like a cloak. Closing in on herself. Unable and unwilling to let any emotions in or out. It seemed the safest and the least tormenting thing to do.

Mezze demolished, Nikos pressed a buzzer beside his plate. Moments later Spiros and the young manservant were back, whisking away the empty plates, depositing new ones along with grilled fish, herbed potatoes, green beans and salads. Then they disappeared again.

As before, she ate steadily, trying not to look at Nikos, trying to shut him out of her consciousness. He was doggedly continuing his monologue about the villa, talking to her in a polite voice that he might use to any welcome guest, seemingly immune to the fact that she was not replying to him as he moved on to telling her about the island and the places of interest on it, then this whole region of the Aegean, and the chain of which this island was a part.

Memory stabbed at her of having dinner with him that unforgettable night they'd met, and how she'd been the very opposite of the way she was being now. Not closed and silent and unsmiling, but she'd opened up to him, drinking him in, face lit, eyes glowing, still half disbelieving that she really was with this incredible man who could melt her with a glance from his long-lashed dark eyes... a glance that had told her of his desire for her and how he wanted the evening to end...

Her jaw tightened, bringing her back to now. *Well, it's ended here, hasn't it? This is where that evening has brought you—to this. Pregnant by a man who doesn't even believe your baby is his, and thinks you're just trying to get your hands on his precious money.*

Bitterness filled her and she felt her throat constrict. It had become painful to swallow. Impossible. She set down her fork, fish unfinished.

He paused, looking across at her. She did not wait for him to speak again, to say anything more, but spoke instead.

'Why am I here, Nikos?'

Her question was direct, and it came not from any conscious decision to speak, yet the words hung between them.

For a moment he did not answer, first reaching for his wine, taking a draught of the ruby liquid glowing in the light of the candles in their sheltering glass holders.

She felt the moment lengthen, knowing her voice had been low and strained. But how could it be anything else? Just hours earlier she had been clawing at him, pummelling him, yelling at him in gasping rage and fury. Yet now they were sharing dinner together under a starry sky, above the quiet lapping of the Aegean Sea, with the low, ceaseless murmur of the cicadas all around.

He set back his wine glass, looked across at her. 'To give you time,' he said. His voice, too, was low. 'Time…' he drew a breath '…to be less angry with me.'

Her expression altered. 'Why should that even be possible?' she answered. There was a bitterness in her voice she could hear herself. 'After what you've accused me of!'

He drew breath again. 'What if I said to you…' he spoke slowly, picking his words with care, and she was aware of it, could see it in the way he looked at her, as carefully as he was speaking to her '…that in Athens last night I got it wrong?'

She did not answer, only waited. And after a moment he went on, still in that careful voice, with that watchful regard, seeing how she would react, she knew.

'And that now,' he said, his eyes never leaving her, 'I am trying to get it right.'

The candle flickered in the night air and she was not sure she could read him. There might be something that she could not see.

'You mean,' she said, knowing that her mouth had twisted, her voice too, 'you no longer think I'm some kind of scheming gold-digger, trying to get her hands on your precious money and scamming you with a baby that isn't even yours!'

She did not bother to hide the expression in her eyes. She saw his face tense.

'I told you. I got it wrong last night. And I'm sorry for it. Which is why—' he took an incised breath '—I want to start over.' He paused, eyes holding hers. Then, 'Alys, we have to get to know each other. We spent one night with each other, but we're still strangers in all other respects, and that is what has to change. For you, for me—for the baby.'

He paused again, and she could see something move in his eyes, but still did not know what.

'Our baby,' he said.

The words fell into the space between them. She wanted to challenge him, to demand whether he believed that—believed what he'd just admitted.

But why would he say it if he doesn't believe it, doesn't acknowledge what I know to be true?

'Give me a chance, Alys.' He was speaking again, his eyes still holding hers across the table, candlelight flickering in their dark depths. 'A chance to mend the mistake I made last night. To get it right instead of wrong. Will you let me do that?'

She did not answer. Could not. Painful thoughts contorted in her head. Last night she'd wanted only to flee Nikos for ever. But now...?

Confusion filled her, and wariness, and uncertainty, and above all an inability to give voice to any answer at all.

It seemed he did not need one. She saw his expression flicker in the candlelight.

'I'll take your silence as consent,' he said. There was dryness in his voice, and wryness.

But she could not answer even that. She was beyond it. Beyond everything. Instead, she picked up her fork, resumed eating her dinner.

After a moment, so did Nikos.

CHAPTER SEVEN

NIKOS LAY IN his bed, staring up the ceiling fan circling slowly.

Had he said the right thing? Had she believed him? It was impossible to tell. Impossible to read her. He would just have to trust that he had convinced her. But at least he was further on than he had been at the airport, with her about to bolt back to England.

Hasten slowly...

Sometimes that was the way forward in a deal. Not to rush the other party. To give them time to feel comfortable.

And that's what she needs to feel.

The way she'd obviously felt with him in London. And he with her.

I need to recapture that—make it real for her again.

He would start tomorrow. Hastening slowly. Getting her exactly where he wanted her to be. *Needed* her to be. Using all the skill he possessed to achieve it.

Alys had retired as soon as they'd finished dinner, and although she hadn't thought she would sleep easily, with so much in her head, she'd slept deeply and peacefully, waking to sunshine slanting thinly through the louvred shutters. She'd dressed quickly in cotton trousers and a short-sleeved shirt, before stepping out onto the bedroom's balcony—which, she now realised, was an extension of the terrace, curving around the entire frontage of the villa.

The morning sun on the sea was dazzling, dancing on tiny wavelets, almost too bright to bear. The air was warm, and sweet with the scent of flowers. Vivid crimson bougainvillea tumbled down the walls, over the balustrade, down the steep garden. Beyond the garden, on the promontory, thin cypresses pierced the azure sky.

She gazed out over it, all so wonderfully beautiful about her. And out of nowhere she felt her spirits lift.

I am here, in this fantastic luxury villa, and for whatever reason I am here I might as well enjoy it!

After all, it would not come again. Soon she would be back in England, finding a job to last until she had her baby, keeping her costs as low as possible while she continued to pay the mortgage—now blessedly not in arrears, with that crushing fear lifted from her. Perhaps she could get a job that would allow her some maternity leave… and she must try and find a childminder too. Because although she had not wanted to be a working mother, now she must be.

Her expression hardened. Whatever her confused thoughts and feelings about what Nikos had said to her last night, she must still be wary. She had let him pay off her arrears, removing the worst of her fears for the future, but that did not mean she would or should let herself be dependent on him for the future of herself and her baby.

Who knows? He might change his mind about me yet again?

That jaundiced, cynical thought was in her head and she would not banish it. Nor let down her guard just because of a few well-spun lines from him about starting over and making amends for what he'd said to her in Athens.

Not yet.

And maybe not ever.

She walked further along the terrace until she reached the section where they had dined, in front of the wide reception room. Nikos was already at the table, now set for breakfast. He got to his feet, courteously coming around to pull back her chair for her. She nodded briefly, sitting down. She was hungry, and the scent of fresh-baked rolls curled around her.

Nikos resumed his place. 'How are you this morning?' he asked. 'You slept well, I hope?'

Alys nodded again, reaching for a roll and a dish of pale butter.

'May I pour you some coffee?' Nikos offered. 'Or perhaps orange juice first?'

'No coffee, thank you, but orange juice will be

lovely,' she said, and he poured it for her as she buttered her roll, then followed it with a spoonful of golden honey.

She focussed on what she was doing, not on Nikos. It was safer that way. And not because she was still closed in on herself, still infinitely wary of what was going on. But because looking at Nikos would mean taking in his physical impact all over again.

He looked different again now, in a pair of cut-off denims and a white tee that moulded his powerful torso in ways she should not, *must* not pay attention to.

She swallowed, helping herself to more orange juice, which refreshed her, so when Nikos, glancing across at her, asked in that careful voice he was using whether she would object to a quiet day at the villa, she felt she could only nod assent.

She kept it at that, starting to eat her honeyed roll, savouring the softness of the fresh bread, the richness of the butter, the sweetness of the honey.

The sun was warm on the back of her head, her neck and shoulders, and she looked around her at the glorious, sun-drenched vista, feeling a sense of blessing from the sheer beauty of the place.

'It's good here, isn't it?' Nikos's voice sounded, quiet against the backdrop of the cicada's ceaseless chorus. 'You can see why I thought it would be the right place for us.'

Her eyes went to him. 'There is no "us", Nikos. There is a baby, but there is no "us".'

There was a tightening in her throat as she spoke. The sense of blessing had vanished. Replaced by all that was between them. All that made his 'us' impossible.

He nodded slowly. 'I won't pressurise you, Alys. What I said is what I meant—that we should simply spend time here. Get used to each other. Get to know each other.'

She looked at him, then dropped her eyes, saying nothing in response, only continuing with her breakfast, looking out over the vista to give herself something to do—and because it was so beautiful to look at.

After a while, Nikos spoke again. In that same courteous, solicitous tone. 'So, after breakfast, would you like to spend the morning by the pool?'

'I didn't bring any swimwear,' Alys heard herself answer.

'No matter—some is always kept here for houseguests. The maids can bring you a selection to choose from.'

'Oh. Well. Thank you.' Her answer felt awkward, but he did not appear to notice.

'Good,' he said. Then frowned. 'You must ensure you have sufficient sun cream, though—protect your pale skin.'

As he spoke, a memory flickered in her head of how he'd laughed as they'd lain entwined in each other's arms, that one single night they'd had, at how her skin was so pale against his Mediterranean tan. She pushed the memory away. There was no place for it here.

He was telling her that the maids would also bring her a selection of sun creams, as well as the swimwear.

'Do you swim?' Nikos asked.

She nodded, glancing down at the stepped pathway winding through the terraced gardens. At the bottom she could see the swimming pool, glistening under the sunshine. It looked dazzlingly inviting...

It looked even more so when, wearing a royal blue one-piece swimsuit whose simplicity did not disguise the fact that it was a very expensive item, as were the blue-patterned wrap that went with it and the blue bead-encrusted flip-flops on her feet, she emerged onto the pool deck. It was semicircular, with the oval pool at its centre, a pool house to one side and a low retaining wall smothered in yet more bougainvillea.

As at breakfast, Nikos was already there. Clearly ready for a morning swim.

Alys felt her stomach hollow. He was propped up on a lounger. Dark green board shorts snaked around his hips and his bronzed torso was bare. Memory flared—memory she did not want, could not stop.

Running my fingertips across his chest, graz-

*ing them over every contour, feeling every honed
muscle beneath my touch, revelling in it, glory-
ing in it—*

She felt colour run up into her cheeks and turned
away to drop down on the lounger set a little way
away from Nikos's.

'Did you put sun cream on?'

His voice made her turn towards him. He was
wearing sunglasses and she could not see his eyes.

'Yes.' She nodded. 'I've brought the bottle down.
And I hope you don't mind… I found some magazines—'

She spoke awkwardly, not actually wanting to
talk, but feeling she ought to, because she'd helped
herself to the magazines. They weren't magazines
she would have chosen, but they were in English,
and presumably they must have more than fashion pages in them.

'There are some English language books on the
lounge bookshelves as well,' he replied. He held up
a paperback with a lurid cover showing two men
shooting at each other, and a speeding car in the
background. 'I found one for myself.' He gave a
half-smile. 'Action adventure—haven't read anything like this in years!'

She didn't smile back, only settled herself on the
lounger, feeling the heat of the sun beating down
on her. She got her own sunglasses out of the bag
and put them on. It gave her some protection. And
not just from the brightness of the Aegean sun.

From Nikos.

She shut her eyes, lying back, thoughts racing. Could she cope with this? Could she really cope with lying here, sunbathing next to Nikos at his luxury villa, going along with what he'd asked of her, and yet all the time being so burningly conscious of him, of how it had been that very first time she'd set eyes on him…

She made herself relax, felt the heat soaking into her, heard cicadas chorusing all round, the sound of Nikos turning a page from time to time, the low lap of the sea on the beaches below.

It was very peaceful. And slowly, very slowly, she began to feel the peace of it too. Without being conscious of it she slid her hand across her abdomen, resting it lightly where, safe and secret within, her precious baby lay. She felt her breathing slow right down, let the chorus of the cicadas fade away, and under the somnolent heat of the sun slipped into drowsing slumber.

Nikos heard her breathing change. Through his dark glasses he glanced towards her. He felt his breath catch. She'd let the beach wrap fall back and now she lay there, arms and shoulders bare, long legs exposed, her still-slender figure moulded by the one-piece. Across her lower abdomen her hand was resting, splayed out. A timeless gesture of protection for an unborn child.

His throat tightened.

How beautiful she looked! Like a sleeping expectant Madonna—mother and child-to-be…

He felt emotion well in him, new and strange. Confusing and conflicted.

For a long, timeless moment he watched her… the slow rise and fall of her breasts, the grace of her body, the beauty of her face…

Then he looked away, back to his book.

But he was paying no attention to it.

Alys rested her hands on the sun-warmed stone of the balustrade edging the terrace, watching the sun turning the world to gold just as she had twenty-four hours ago.

And just as *he* had twenty-four hours ago, Nikos was strolling up to her, a tumbler of pomegranate juice in one hand, a beer glass for himself in the other. He handed the former to her and she took a sip, her eyes going back to the gold-lit vista all around.

'So, has it been a good day, do you think?'

Nikos's enquiry was quietly spoken and she glanced at him. Nodded slowly.

'I'm glad,' he said. He paused. Then, 'So, do you think you prefer the beach to the pool, or the other way around?'

His enquiry was polite, and Alys heard herself answer, because a nod would not work to answer his question. 'They're both beautiful. The whole place is beautiful,' she said, her voice low.

She let her gaze slip out towards the panorama. Down below, to her right-hand side, she could get a glimpse through the greenery of the small curve of sand and shingle that was the tiny beach they'd gone down to that afternoon. Lunch had been served on the pool deck, a light al fresco affair of fresh bread and cheeses, charcuterie and sweet tomatoes, and sweeter peaches.

Easy to consume, and easy for Nikos to make his unfailing one-sided conversation over. Just as he was doing now, making some remark about sea swimming. He'd done just that after they'd settled on the beach, and she'd watched him run lithely into the lapping water, arch his incredible body and launch himself into the deeper water, then swim vigorously away from the shore in a strong, powerful freestyle, splashing up diamonds in the sunshine as he ploughed forward.

He'd returned some time later, hair slicked back, those same diamonds glancing off his body as he'd reached for a towel, padding himself dry. He'd been grinning, visibly exhilarated, and then he had thrown himself down to dry off completely in the sun.

Alys had looked out to sea again, because that had been easier than looking at his near-naked body bringing memories she must not have...

She felt her stomach hollow again, her eyes going to Nikos in chinos and an open-necked shirt with turned-back cuffs, his hair freshly washed and feathering at the nape of his neck. He was freshly shaved too, it seemed, judging by his pristine jawline.

Wariness prickled in her veins. She should steel herself against him, warn herself that he might turn on her again, as he had in Athens…

And yet all day long Nikos had done nothing except treat her as if she were made of porcelain, endlessly solicitous, painstakingly courteous. He was still doing that now, asking her if, tomorrow, she might like to try going out on the water.

'There's a choice of sail or motor,' he said. 'Which would you prefer?'

'I've never tried either,' she answered.

'Then we'll see what the wind conditions are like tomorrow. Too light, and the dinghy won't get us anywhere. Too brisk, and it could get a bit bumpy.'

There was a sound behind them and he turned. It was one of the maids, lighting the candles on the table, which was set for dinner again. As she left, Nikos thanked her.

Alys could hear the word *efharisto*, and something more, and she saw how the girl flushed with pleasure and hurried off. A tiny, brief vignette, and yet her gaze flickered. It showed that she herself was not the only female whose head would turn at Nikos's glance, warm to his smile.

They took their places at the table, with dusk melting into night, and somehow, despite all her wariness, all her holding back from him, and perhaps because of the day they'd spent in each other's company, Alys found herself replying in the face of Nikos's continued punctilious politeness towards her.

Just little things—a question that came to her from something he'd said about tourism on the island…an observation of her own. Not much, and not often, but she did it all the same.

The food was once again delicious, served by Spiros and the young manservant—Spiros's nephew Andreas, Nikos told her with a smile. Alys smilingly praised the food—chicken tonight, in a light, lemony sauce, with delicate rice and grilled courgettes, following on from a layered seafood terrine in a lobster bisque.

She ate with a will—not just because the sun and sea air seemed to have given her an appetite, but to make the most of this brief spell of indolent and pampered luxury.

Make the most of being here with Nikos.

She froze, her fork motionless in mid-air. Where had that come from? That totally out of place, irrelevant and untrue thought?

Her eyes went across to him as he tucked into the delicious dish. Something kicked through her—something about the angle of his head, the way his shirt collar framed his sinewed neck, the way his long, strong fingers pressed the blade of the knife into the tender chicken breast…something about the way his thick, dark lashes dipped down over his deep brown eyes as he ate…something that she was suddenly aware was quickening her pulse, making her feel her heart thud in her chest, emotion build within her.

Just from looking at him.

Being with him…

'Alys?'

She heard her name spoken, a note of concern in it.

'Are you all right?'

She nodded—a hasty gesture. 'Yes, thank you. It was nothing.'

Because 'nothing' is all I can ever allow myself to feel about Nikos. Even if he does now believe my baby is his, that does not mean there can be anything between us. If he has any concern it will be about the baby. Not about me.

His next words, when he spoke, echoed just that. She could hear the same note of concern in his voice—but it was not for her.

'The obstetrician told me you were progressing well—that you had no health problems, had reported none and he could see none.' He was frowning slightly as he spoke, his eyes searching her face. 'But I wondered just now, when you stopped eating, if maybe—'

She drew a breath. 'I'm fine,' she said. 'Completely healthy.'

His eyes were still on her. 'You hardly show yet,' he said.

'I'm not as slim as I was,' she answered.

Then, immediately, she wished she had said nothing in response. Nikos's gaze was now flickering over her.

Out of the meagre wardrobe she'd brought with her to Greece she was wearing the knee-length denim skirt again, but a different top this time—one that, she realised now, with a flush, had become tighter since the previous summer. It moulded her breasts, outlining them. Was he seeing that?

She hunched forward to minimise the effect. She must change the subject...think of something innocuous to say. But Nikos spoke first.

'You look,' he said slowly, 'radiant.'

Her eyes went to his. There was something in them that made her reel.

'They say pregnant women have a glow about them, and in you I can absolutely see why.'

She swallowed. 'I caught the sun today, that's all,' she said. She reached for her iced water, needing its chill.

He shook his head. 'It's more than that,' he said, in the same slow manner, as if he were realising it for the first time. 'You're more beautiful than ever, Alys.'

There was a huskiness in his voice, colour in his cheeks...

'Don't!'

The word came automatically to her. Negating what he was saying. She took a mouthful of water, cold to her throat.

He gave a slow shake of his head. 'You make it very hard, Alys,' he said.

She could feel the heat beating up into her cheeks, the quickening of her heart rate. She wanted it to stop. Wanted this whole moment to stop—just stop.

She looked away, felt a churning inside her. Then, to her relief, he began saying something else. Something about taking the motorboat out the next day, where they might visit in it. She was glad—and grateful. She answered him in kind, getting past the impossible moment that was now thankfully gone.

Because I can't have it! It's got no place between us. Not any more!

She heard herself ask something about how fast the motorboat could travel…could it reach the other islands in the group clustering in this part of the Aegean? The subject was so much more bearable than what he had tried to talk about.

Before long they had finished their main course, and Spiros and Andreas were there again, bestowing upon them a creamy peach bavarois that slipped down her throat like balm, followed by coffee served Greek-style for Nikos and a herbal tea for herself.

Not wanting to go anywhere near what he had said earlier, she asked him about Greek coffee, hearing in return how it was derived from the way the Turks had introduced it, which led on to the time of the Ottoman occupation, and the long, dark centuries of conquest and occupation by the Sultan's forces.

He spoke with passion and feeling, regaling her with the history she knew only dimly herself.

'That must go very deep into the modern Greek psyche,' she heard herself saying, looking across at him.

A thought struck her, making her wonder. *Will my baby share that too?*

Her eyes rested on Nikos. His face was animated by what he was telling her.

Will he—or she—look like him as well? Share those dark, devastating looks of his?

She silenced the questions. What would it matter? Her baby would grow up without Nikos in its life. Grow up without a father. As she had had to.

Unless...

Did it have to be like that? She had been forced to think so, resign herself to it, after he'd revealed his ugly condemnation of her. Now, though, he had told her he accepted her baby as his—did the rest of his condemnation of her still hold?

Does he still think all I want is his money?

After all, hadn't she justified his low opinion of her by letting him pay off her mortgage arrears as

she had? She could tell herself all she liked that
any court would impose maintenance demands on
him, but how did that avoid his accusation that she
wanted to profit from her pregnancy?

So would she want him in her baby's life, thinking that of her?

Surely there could be only one sane answer
to that.

In her head, as she sat listening to Nikos telling
her the tale of the struggle for Greek independence,
she heard the echo of her own voice at breakfast.

'There is no "us", Nikos.'

It went on echoing.

CHAPTER EIGHT

NIKOS OPENED THE throttle of the sleek motorboat and it thrust forward with a powerful roar of the outboard engine. He gave a laugh—a carefree sound. He couldn't even remember the last time he'd taken a motorboat out like this, and certainly not here at the Villa Drakis, where he hadn't been for years.

He felt himself frown. Had his life really been restricted to endless business trips abroad to do endless deals to make ever more money for the Drakis coffers? Only snatching brief time off to spend a weekend every now and then with the likes of sophisticated females like Irinia, wining and dining them in Michelin-starred restaurants in snatches before flying off yet again, or heading back to Athens to report to his father, set up yet another potential money-making deal, and then be off again?

He shook his mind free of such thoughts, focussing on the here and now—on what was now essential to him: putting everything else about his life totally aside and focussing on the woman who was so totally unlike all the Irinias of this world—who was changing everything in his life.

Changing it for ever.

And I have to get it right! Far too much is at stake.

And surely now, after his initial near-catastrophic miscalculation, he was beginning to do so? Though it was slow going with Alys, she was finally progressing beyond mere nods and monosyllables. He was on the right track with her. Yesterday had been good—today would be better.

Bringing her here to the villa had been exactly the right thing to do. Slowly, but inexorably, she was responding to his new treatment of her, letting go of the hostility that his previous harshness had engendered.

And it must not come back. That's essential!

It was more than essential.

Because I don't want to feel hostile to her either.

He heard an echo of his words to her over dinner last night. *'You look radiant.'*

He turned to look at Alys now, sitting by the gunwale, her hair streaming like a flag in the wind, her face in profile lifted to the sun and the wind. How beautiful she was…

He dragged his gaze back to the sea. They were heading parallel to the rocky shoreline of the promontory, and before long had cleared it to starboard and made a wide, circling manoeuvre out to sea.

He pointed to the rounded tip of the promontory, turning to Alys from the wheel. 'Can you see? Right at the very tip there's a cove, a sandy beach. You can only reach it by sea. That's where we're heading.'

He steered towards it, reducing speed as the water became shallower and calmer, became turquoise. Moments later he was cutting the engine, lifting the motor out of the water, dropping anchor.

'Time for our picnic,' he said. He knew his voice was cheerful, enthusiastic, still infused with the sense of being carefree that had come over him as he'd let rip with the motorboat.

He hefted up the wicker picnic basket and chill box and jumped down into the shallow water, splashing to shore and depositing his burdens in the shade of a large rock. Then he came back for Alys. She was standing up, beach bag and towels in hand, about to jump into the ankle-deep water.

Instead of letting her do so, Nikos reached out his hands, put them around her waist, swinging her down. She was as light as a feather, but he could feel her whole body stiffen before he lowered her onto the sand, feeling the warmth of her body in his hands.

She went to the picnic things, busying herself deliberately, or so he fancied, then getting a towel, flapping it down on the sand, placing her beach bag on it to weigh it down. She was wearing the one-piece suit again, with a tee shirt over it today—

stronger protection against the midday sun than a flimsy wrap.

'We'll rehydrate, then catch a swim before lunch,' Nikos declared.

He hunkered down to click open the chill box and extract a plastic bottle of mineral water, cold to the touch. He handed it to Alys, taking another one for himself. Then he straightened, unscrewing the top and taking a good few gulps, making sure she did as well.

'OK, let's hit the water.'

He waited for her and, as she stepped gingerly over the hot sand, took her hand to help her. He felt her try to yank it back, but would not let her.

'I don't want you stumbling,' he told her.

It was strange to hold her hand, however briefly. Strange and very good.

When they gained the lapping edge of the sea she extricated her hand. His felt empty suddenly.

'Leave your tee shirt on,' he recommended. 'You can burn just as badly in the water. In you go.'

Carefully, she waded in beside him, going as deep as her waist. She seemed to hesitate a moment, then she pushed off into a gentle breaststroke, her tee shirt billowing out above her shoulders as she did so.

He came up beside her. 'Nice?' he asked.

She nodded.

'It won't get deep till you're quite far out.' He gave her another smile. 'I'm going to work up an appetite!' he said lightly, and plunged in with a duck dive.

He surfaced ten metres out, after dolphin kicks under water. Then he took off in an energetic free-style. As it had the day before, it exhilarated him. He headed straight out, felt the swell increase with the depth of the water, and turned to head back inshore. Alys was now sitting in the shallows, the wet tee shirt clinging to her body. Outlining her breasts. Her crested nipples.

He stopped short. Arousal, out of nowhere, surged in him. Thank God he was still over his waist in water. He fought for control. But it took an effort he could barely make. Did not want to make.

Because what he wanted was to—

No. He slammed the brakes down. Hard. With gritted teeth, he ground out his maxim to himself.

Hasten slowly—with the whole emphasis on slowly, dammit!

He was barely two days out from bringing her here. And no way was she ready yet.

But I have to get her there. Have to get her to exactly where I want her...need her...to be.

He drew a breath, conscious that his heart was pounding—and not just from the exertion of his vigorous swim. He slicked his hands through his hair, wading towards her, water splashing around his thighs.

She'd knotted her hair loosely on top of her head, but fronds had tendrilled around her face. Sunshine kissed her skin, flushed from yesterday's sunbathing, like a honeyed peach.

Emotion caught at him—or something did. Something that was not the urgent arousal that had surged in him so overpoweringly just now. Something else. Something that was more like what he'd felt yesterday, watching her sleeping by the pool, a recumbent Madonna, dreaming of the child she was to bear. Something that seemed to join the two together—the erotic charge of the first with the wonder of the second. Something that met and melded with them both.

He hunkered down beside her, his breathing easing now, his elevated heart rate recovering from his exertions, holding out a hand to her.

'I'm starving. Let's see what's in the picnic box.'

She curled her legs under her to propel herself upright. Nikos kept his hand out. There was a moment's hesitancy, then she put her hand in his, to let him draw her effortlessly to her feet.

He wanted to punch the air in triumph. But he did not push the moment, letting her go and heading across to the shade of the rock, throwing himself down on the towel and flipping open the cool box. Getting out the water bottles, he handed one to Alys as she came up, then lowered herself cross-legged to her own towel. As she started to drink thirstily her hand moved across her lower stomach—the same gesture she'd made yesterday by the pool. It was becoming familiar to him. More than familiar…

Emotions flickered in him like a faulty electrical circuit that was uncertain of the connections it needed to make it flow properly.

He slugged down the rest of the water, then reached for a beer, making inroads on that too, before undoing the wicker picnic basket. It was brim-full of goodies, and his stomach growled.

'Dig in,' he invited, starting to spread out the feast: cold chicken, cold salmon, prawns and crayfish, cheeses and hams and ready-mixed salads, fresh rolls and butter and salad dressing, a meltingly flaky filo pastry pie and tomatoes the size of apples.

Eating was messy and informal. Nikos lounged back on one elbow, and Alys stayed in her flexible legs-crossed position as they worked their way through the repast. Nikos kept up a flow of easygoing conversation, as he had become used to, making all the running, getting only occasional replies from Alys.

He'd never had to make the running when it came to women—they never held out against him, were always eager for his attentions. As Alys had been that first night together.

Yet now…

To get even the suggestion of a smile out of her was an achievement. That wariness, that withdrawal into herself, keeping him at bay, was still paramount. Oh, she was lowering her guard against him, but he could take nothing for granted. Nothing.

A thought came to him—one that struck him out of nowhere.

What if I hadn't left her that morning in London?

He stilled a moment, letting it sink into him. What if he'd cancelled those damn appointments in the City? Never flown off to Geneva that day to talk to yet another bunch of private bankers? If, instead, he'd taken off with Alys, fresh from his bed, to somewhere much, much more enticing. The Caribbean, the Maldives, the Seychelles...

Just her and me taking off together. Being together like we are here, now. Carefree, enjoying ourselves. Enjoying life, enjoying being with each other...

It was a powerful thought. One he could not dismiss. Did not wish to...

His eyes rested on her. She was eating one of the giant tomatoes and a thread of juice was running down her chin. He wanted to lean forward and lick it away, move his lips up to her mouth, open it to his...

He reached for a slice of the filo pie, to distract himself from thoughts that could bear no fruit. Not yet...

Picnic finished, he watched her pack the remains away, make use of the scented handwipes provided, then he settled himself back on his towel, reminding Alys she needed to top up her sunblock. He folded his arms under his head, watching her do just as he'd told her, liking the way her hands smoothed down over her long legs in wide, sensual strokes. Wanting to do it for her...

Then she was done, lying back as he was doing, the tee shirt, quite dry now, protecting her torso.

He gazed upwards into the cerulean sky, avoiding the sun. Thoughts circled in his head. That first night here, at dinner, he'd said 'our baby'. He'd said it because he'd known she needed to hear it or she would make it impossible for him to achieve what he must achieve with her.

But hadn't he needed to hear it too?

Do I really believe that she fell from my bed into another man's, or came to my bed from another man's? Do I truly believe that of her?

Yes, he had seen her and swept her into his bed in a single night, but did that mean she made a habit of such things? He himself did not—so why should he think it of her?

And, for all the way she'd been glitzed to the nines, when he'd taken her to bed she had not been some highly experienced sexual sophisticate at all—ardent, yes, but with a sweetness and eagerness that had captivated him. And in the morning, watching her sleeping, he had seen an innocence about her that had told him their night together had been as rare for her as it had for him...

He levered himself up on his elbow to look down

on her as she lay, eyes closed, breathing gently. Whether she was asleep or not he did not know. All he knew was that she had looked just like that as he'd gazed down on her sleeping figure that morning in London, when he'd left her. And she was filling him with the same desire... A desire that surely could only prove one thing...

How could I desire her believing she carries another man's child? It would be impossible.

Yet desire was what he felt now—strong and insistent. Just as he had in that moment of arousal as he'd watched her, lolling in the water, her nipples cresting beneath the wet fabric of her tee shirt. It was his own body telling him the truth about her...

About myself...

As if she'd sensed him gazing down at her, she opened her eyes, meeting his. For an instant, a moment of time so brief it might not have existed, something moved in their depths—and then it was gone. Shuttered out.

'What is it? Why do you look at me like that?'

There was defensiveness in her voice—he could hear it. He did not want it there. Needed to banish it.

He spoke slowly, almost haltingly. 'I was remembering how I looked down at you that morning in London, asleep in bed, knowing I had to leave you.' He paused. 'Not wanting to.' His expression changed, shadowed. 'I thought I had to leave you. That it was the only prudent thing to do. Thought that what we'd had was…' he took a heavy breath '…a one-off encounter. That I should walk away and leave it like that. But—'

He stopped, his eyes switching to the azure sea, to the far horizon where it merged with the sky. It was impossible to tell which was which. Impossible to know where the boundary was.

Like the boundary between that night with Alys and the reality of my life, where work dominates and only women like Irinia give me any respite.

His gaze dropped down again, meeting her eyes, still shuttered as they were to him. He knew he needed to tell her this. Wanted to tell her.

'I came back for you—I came back to London to find you.'

The words fell from him before he could stop them, consider them…decide whether they were the right words to say. He didn't care. He wanted to say them. Wanted Alys to hear them.

'I realised I didn't want just one night with you. So I came back to find you. I went to the hotel and then—' He broke off.

There was a moment's silence.

'Then the concierge gave you the letter I'd left for you.' Alys's voice supplied the answer. It was expressionless.

He took another breath. 'Yes. And then…' He paused again, feeling that breath tight in his lungs. 'Then it all went wrong,' he said. 'But now…' His expression changed again. 'Now all I want is to get it right. Not just because of the baby. But between *us*, Alys.'

Alys sat on the gunwale of the motorboat, as she had that morning on the trip out. Nikos was going more slowly now, gently bobbing across water that was turning to gold with the lowering sun. Her eyes went to him. His hair was wind-ruffled, eyes masked by his sunglasses, his bronzed, leanly muscled torso lit with the golden sun.

His words to her, as she'd lain there on the beach, with him gazing down on her, burned in her mind. *'All I want is to get it right...between us,'* he'd said.

Then her own words to him of the night before slammed over them. *'There is no "us", Nikos.'*

She heard them both, playing and replaying in her head. Impossible to reconcile. Her eyes lifted to the approaching shoreline, to the white villa above the bougainvillea-laced terraced gardens, landscaped into the steep slope.

Just imagine living here.

She yanked the thought away. No, that was not possible—not permissible. She was simply passing through, that was all.

Yet she felt a pang for all that. She could grow to love this place...

What if there were an 'us' between Nikos and me?

The thought was in her head, taking form

and shape. Becoming reality. Bringing others in its wake.

He said he came back to London to find me... What if I had not left that letter for him, or if I had never conceived that night...?

She pulled her thoughts away. It had not happened like that. It had happened the way it had, and that was why she was here now—for no other reason. Not because there was any 'us' between her and Nikos.

There was only a baby yoking them together, and everything about the future was still...uncertain.

That was all she must remember.

Yet once the boat was docked and moored, as she and Nikos made their slow ascent up the steps to the terrace, she heard his words in her head again.

'I came back for you...'

And she felt a strange and hopeless ache form inside her...

CHAPTER NINE

DINNER THAT EVENING, after their second full day with each other at the villa, seemed easier. Conversation seemed easier. Just being with Nikos seemed easier.

He drew no attention to it, and Alys was glad. That made it easier too: easier to respond to what he was saying, to make replies, ask questions, almost to have a conversation with him.

She didn't want to examine it, or analyse it, or question it. All she wanted was to let it be as it was: feeling easier.

There was the same atmosphere at breakfast the next day too. As she took one of an array of freshly baked rolls, reaching for the butter and honey, Nikos smiled across at her.

'How about if I show you something of the island today? We could take off after breakfast, if you like, and maybe have lunch in town if that appeals?'

She nodded, but it was not to avoid replying verbally. 'Thank you—that would be nice,' she said.

Was there less constraint in her voice? She thought there was. It seemed to be part of this 'easier' that she was so conscious of.

Easier not to perpetually be on her guard against him, to be wary of him, withdrawing into herself, speaking as little as she could. Easier to acquiesce, to let his solicitousness continue, to reply rather than only nod when he spoke to her, to be complaisant and agree to his suggestions—like she was now, about going out. Because, after all, why not?

He smiled, nodding in return. 'Good,' he said, and reached for the coffee pot.

They set off late morning—breakfast had been leisurely—and the high wheel base of the SUV afforded a good view over the countryside and coastline. Conscious that she had seen nothing of either on the drive from the airport, her eyes doggedly shut throughout, her mind too battered and exhausted to pay attention to anything, Alys looked about her now with interest.

The hilly, rugged interior of the island was mostly dry, with olive groves on the lower slopes and maquis interspersed with tall cypress trees. Nikos chatted casually, telling her about what they were seeing, pointing to a radio and communications mast on one of the rocky peaks. Modern windmills were also noticeable in places, reducing the island's dependence, he told her, on imported power. They passed through some coastal fishing villages, then gained the outskirts of the island's small capital.

'What would you like to see first?' Nikos enquired. 'There's an old harbour, but it's a bit touristy as I recall. The marina beyond the ferry dock is more upmarket, and more modern.'

'Could we start at the harbour?' Alys asked. 'Touristy' was, after all, more her natural *milieu*—not a marina stuffed with private yachts.

It wasn't Nikos's, though, that was obvious.

He parked the massive SUV half on the pavement of a side street, and it looked out of place amidst the run-of-the-mill hire cars belonging to the tourists and those owned by the locals. So did Nikos himself.

She glanced at him. Though he was casually dressed, in chinos and an open-necked shirt, he didn't look like a tourist. He looked…

Expensive. Those casual clothes he wears with such effortless elegance cost a fortune, and his sunglasses likewise, and the thin, exclusive-looking gold watch around his wrist! Everything about him just says money. Wealth.

It was a disturbing thought, somehow. Disturbing in its implications.

I shouldn't wonder that he's so suspicious of me, thinking that I've told him about the baby, claimed it's his, because I want to get some of his wealth for myself?

After all, what if she *were* what he had accused

her of being, doing what he was accusing her of trying to do? She rallied her thoughts, fighting them off.

Did he still think that?

He believes the baby is his. That, surely, has to be a start.

Her face shadowed. The start of what?

Nikos had talked of 'us', but there was no 'us', nor could there be.

Weariness washed through her, and a deep, deep reluctance to wade back into such turbid, toxic waters.

She looked about her, focussing on the busy scene, taking pleasure in it and putting aside—for now, at least—the impossibility of her situation and the tangle of sharing a child with a man like Nikos Drakis. The situation was fraught with doubts and demands, mistrust and hostility, but now it seemed this tentative, fragile, careful almost-truce was allowing them to be civil to each other, to learn not to be strangers...

As she walked beside him, their pace unhurried, they must look, she realised, just like any other couple strolling along.

'I came back to London to find you,' he had said to her on the beach in that secret cove yesterday. *'I wanted more than one night with you.'*

She felt emotion clench inside her. If that were true, and if she had not fallen pregnant, had never needed to leave that fateful letter for him, would she now be with him? The two of them together as lovers?

The thought pierced her—but what was the use of thinking it? It hadn't happened that way. And even if it had it would not have lasted. It would have been only an affair and then he would have moved on, back to his own world, a world of money and wealth a million miles removed from her own reality.

She felt again the strange ache that had come out of nowhere yesterday, as she thought of might-have-beens that never had been and then set them aside. What else was to be done with them? They had no place in her life.

They were approaching the harbour, which was typical of a thousand others dotted around the Aegean coastline, familiar from travel programmes and postcards. Fishing boats and tourist expedition boats bobbed at their moorings and the quayside was lined with tavernas, their shaded seating areas overlooking the water, their kitchens across the cobbled roadway. The air was filled with appetising smells, and breakfast suddenly seemed a long time ago.

'Can we have lunch here?' she heard herself ask Nikos.

She saw him glance dismissively down the row of tavernas.

'There'll be better fare at the marina restaurants,' he answered.

But she did not want to sit in some sleek, expensive restaurant, feeling out of place, knowing she was only there because she was the one-night stand of a rich man who'd ended up pregnant by him.

'Here looks more fun,' she countered. 'How about this one?'

It looked cheerful, with blue-checked paper tablecloths and a striped awning, and it was already filling up with customers.

Nikos was looking at her. 'Would you really prefer here to the marina?' he asked.

She nodded. 'This is me, Nikos. My world. And...' she looked at him straight '... I'm quite happy with it.'

Without waiting for a response, nor wanting him to insist on the upmarket marina, she turned to the waiter allocating tables.

'For two?' she asked, pointing to herself and Nikos, then at a table right by the water. 'That one?' she said hopefully.

She sat down happily, feeling comfortable there, and flicked open the menu the waiter had hurriedly handed her.

'Tourist fare,' said Nikos, hardly glancing at his.

A tiny smile hovered at her mouth. 'You'll survive,' she said dryly.

A reluctant laugh broke from him, and he raised a hand in surrender. 'You win,' he said. And then his eyes were on her, even though she couldn't see them through the designer shades covering them. 'It's worth it just to see you smile…'

For a second, she looked at him. She couldn't see his eyes yet she knew she was holding his, and he hers. Something seemed to be holding them together…

Then the waiter was there again, to take their drinks order, and Nikos was ordering beer for himself, asking what juices were available for Alys, relaying them to her in English. She chose a fizzy apple juice and mineral water and the waiter scurried off, just as another one deposited a woven basket of roughly sliced hunks of bread with a few butter pats down on the paper tablecloth.

She looked at her menu, felt herself start to relax, to feel at home here in this tourists' taverna, hearing the mix of languages around her. Maybe it was because everyone around her was relaxed as well—here on holiday, intent on enjoying themselves.

The waiter was back with their drinks, ready to take their food order, and then he disappeared again. Alys sipped her fizzy apple juice, and Nikos took a ruminative mouthful of his beer. It seemed to be a signal to himself to resign himself to his fate in eating at so lowly an eatery, and Alys saw him sit back, stretch out his long legs, take another mouthful of beer before setting it back down again.

She wanted to let her gaze linger on him but

would not allow herself to do so. Instead, she gazed out over the harbour.

'Where does the ferry go to?' she asked, just for something to say, seeing the large ship nosing away from the wide quay beyond the harbour wall.

'It will call at the other islands in this group and circle back round. It will make connections with other ferry routes that would eventually take you back to Athens. All of Greece is connectable by sea—sometimes more so than by land.'

Alys looked at him. 'Do you ever use the ferries?' she asked.

He shook his head. 'The Drakis yacht is moored at Piraeus—the port of Athens.'

He paused, and Alys knew he was looking at her from behind his expensive sunglasses.

'I could have it brought here, if you want, Alys.'

She shook her head. 'No yachts, Nikos,' she said quietly.

'And no upmarket restaurant at the marina either?' he replied. 'Just this tourist taverna instead?'

'Yes,' she answered, and looked away again, out over the harbour at the water dazzling in the sunshine. Making her blink. Or something was.

There was a sudden touch, as light as it was brief, on her hand lying on the paper tablecloth. 'I'm sorry, that was unfair of me. Unkind.'

Nikos's voice was low, and its tone was different from the way he'd spoken before. Alys swallowed.

'But understandable,' she said. She looked

across at him, half glad she couldn't see his eyes, half wishing she could. But not really wanting to see what was probably in them.

She gave a sigh. 'I can't prove to you that I am not what you assumed I was that horrible night in Athens, Nikos,' she said. 'And nor do I see any need to do so.' Her voice was edged. 'It was you who brought me here, remember. I would have returned to England, never to trouble you again—'

'No.'

The word was strongly spoken, and sharply too.

Alys tensed. 'I'll be going back anyway, Nikos, when you've decided you've had enough of me being here.' She kept her eyes on him, though she still could not see his. 'I'm glad you've accepted that the baby is yours,' she said steadily, 'but it doesn't change anything. I'm going to be living in England, and I won't be making any financial demands of you at all. You can put funds aside for college fees or whatever later on, if you want to— but for myself I need nothing. You've paid off my debts, and for that I am truly grateful, but from now on I neither need nor want any of your money.'

She saw his expression tighten.

'You cannot possibly mean that,' he said slowly.

She gave a half-shrug. 'Why not? My mother raised me single-handed, so I can do likewise with my child. There'll be some state support to begin with, and then, like my mother, I'll use a mix of childcare and flexible working around the school calendar when the time comes.'

He frowned. 'What happened to your father?' His question was abrupt.

Alys gave another shrug. 'He wasn't around. He—he didn't know about me.' She looked away, out over the harbour. The bright sunshine dazzling on the water made her blink again.

She heard Nikos speaking, but did not look back at him.

'So because you grew up without a father you think that's OK for our baby too, do you?'

Was there challenge in his voice? Criticism? She didn't know or care. She gave yet another shrug but did not answer. Suddenly, she could not…

To her relief—because it *was* relief, surely?— the arrival of the waiter, as harassed as ever, allowed her to look back. He was depositing large plates of food hurriedly down on their table, and Nikos was absently thanking him before he scurried off again.

Alys picked up her fork, took her chicken souvlaki off the skewer and got stuck in. Eating was preferable to talking if the subject was going to be a difficult one. So she'd better stick to easy ones.

'This is good,' she said, taking another mouthful.

She didn't want Nikos resuming a subject she had no intention of discussing with him. Yet his words echoed in her head, and her own unspoken retort too.

No, I don't think it's OK. But it's not as bad as having a father who thinks the mother of his child is an avaricious gold-digger, hell-bent on getting her hands on all his money courtesy of her baby!

But what use was there in telling him that? He could think what he liked of her.

Defiantly, she went on eating.

Without enthusiasm, Nikos started on his tourist fare. But the pork was surprisingly tasty, the fried potatoes crisp, the beans in their tomato sauce peppery, and it was all washed down well by his beer. With a better will than he'd expected, he worked his way to a clear plate, mopping the remaining juices with a couple of hunks of fresh bread.

He made no attempt at conversation while he ate, but his mind was occupied. His own words echoed.

She can't possibly be genuine in her ridiculous assertion of not taking any child maintenance from me! Is it just some line she's trotting out for my benefit? But if so, what benefit? Why say it at all?

Maybe it was just virtue signalling.

But to what purpose? She didn't need to be virtuous to extract generous financial support from him!

Not that that was going to happen.

More words echoed in his head, from that ugly scene in Athens that evening.

'No child of mine will be born a bastard.'

He felt his fingers grip tightly onto his knife and fork and forced them to relax. Alys would not be returning to England, and she would not be raising his child as a working single mother.

He had very different plans for her.

His gaze went to her, his mood improving automatically. Even dressed as she was, in cheap clothes, without a scrap of make-up, and with her hair simply drawn back into a ponytail, she still looked breathtakingly beautiful.

Radiant.

The word he'd used to describe her over dinner came again, as true now as then, washing away the tension that had flared between them as they'd ventured into difficult waters. It had been his fault, he acknowledged, baiting her with that line about having the Drakis yacht sailed over, tempting her with yet more of the wealth he could offer her…

He would make amends…lighten the atmosphere.

She was just finishing off her own meal, and as she pushed her empty plate aside, dabbing her mouth with her paper serviette, he reached for an uneaten hunk of bread.

'Watch,' he told her.

Their table was right by the water's edge, and near them there was a strip of water between two fishing boats, bobbing either side. Darting about in the clear water were small silvery fishes. He made sure Alys could see them too, then crumbled the bread into the water.

He heard her give a gasp and laughed. The placid-looking fishes had turned into a seething ball of feeding frenzy, devouring the crumbs.

'I used to do that when I was very young,' he heard himself say. 'It never failed to delight me.'

'Was that with your mother?' Alys asked. There was curiosity in her voice.

'No, a nursemaid.' He kept his voice casual. He frowned. 'I think that particular one was called Maria. Or maybe it was Tonia. They changed pretty often.'

He was aware that Alys was looking at him. Aware that he was cursing himself for having opened such a subject.

'Did your own mother not look after you at all?'

It was an enquiry that was very carefully voiced.

'No,' he said. He didn't want to say any more.

He saw that Alys was frowning, and he wanted to change the subject, but she had started to speak again.

'Did she work?' she asked. 'I mean, not out of financial necessity, but to have a career?'

His mouth twisted. He could not stop it. 'Her "career" was spending money,' he said shortly.

He could feel Alys's gaze on him. Didn't want it to be.

He reached for his beer, drained it. 'Then she

took off for California, to continue doing so with her divorce settlement,' he said.

His grip on the empty beer glass tightened. Why the hell was he telling her this? He could see Alys open her mouth, about to say something, but he didn't want to hear it. He turned to summon the waiter imperiously, ignoring the fact that the man was laden down with full plates for other customers and indicating to him that he wanted the bill.

It came promptly, but Nikos could not be bothered to wait either for a credit card swipe or change, and simply put down an excess amount in notes and got to his feet. Alys did likewise.

'What would you like to do now?' Nikos asked as they made their way back onto the street. Alys was pausing, he saw, to nod and say *efharisto* to the harassed waiter, who smiled gratefully in return. Or perhaps he just smiled because what man would *not* smile back at so beautiful a woman?

Instinctively Nikos felt his hand reach for her elbow, guiding her across the roadway to the pavement beyond. A mark of possession, he knew. Primitive, but undeniable.

She carries my child—of course I feel possessive.

He paused when she did, looking about her.

'Could we just explore a little?' she asked. 'Wander around a bit?'

'Of course,' he agreed smoothly. After all, this entire enterprise was about making Alys feel comfortable about being here with him. 'How about up that street?' he suggested, pointing to a narrow cobbled lane lined with souvenir shops. It looked quaint in a touristy sort of way.

They strolled along, threading their way amongst other tourists doing likewise, with Alys pausing frequently to look at the wares set out on displays outside the shops. At one point she examined some ceramic jugs and bowls, glazed in the brilliant blue that was always to be found in such places, with the name of the town and the island on the base. Nikos could see she looked tempted, and was about to offer to buy one of each for her, but she replaced them and moved on.

'Didn't you like them?' he heard himself asking.

'Yes, but they're souvenirs,' she answered.

Nikos frowned faintly. 'So?'

She gave a shrug. 'I'm not exactly on holiday, Nikos,' she said, her voice dry.

Then she pointed across the narrow street towards a shop whose window displayed beachwear. Its doorway was hung with flounced skirts and patterned sundresses, and racks of sandals were set on the pavement.

'Actually, what I do need is some more clothes. Not much—just a couple of things more suitable for here than what I brought with me from England for Athens.'

Nikos glanced dismissively at the shop she was pointing at. 'There are some boutiques in the marina,' he said. 'You'll do much better there.'

She shook her head. 'This place is fine, Nikos.'

She made her way across, and he followed reluctantly. Pausing only to skim the shoes and grab a pair of plastic flip-flops, she disappeared inside, busying herself riffling through the packed racks of clothes, extracting some items swiftly. She looked through a pile of tee shirts, helping herself to a couple, picked up a pair of pale blue cotton shorts, then seized a yellow cotton peasant-style skirt with embroidery around the hem, and a flower-sprigged top in light green.

She took them to the till, but Nikos tried to get there before her, silently extracting his credit card. The cashier was already placing Alys's purchases into a pair of carrier bags, taking the debit card that Alys was holding out to her.

'Allow me,' he said. Though his voice was smooth, he could hear an underlying edge in it. Knew why it was there.

Alys ignored him, keying in her pin, then removing her card, tucking it back into her handbag, thanking the cashier and taking the carrier bags.

Slowly, Nikos put his credit card away. Followed her out of the shop.

On the pavement, Alys turned. Chin lifted. 'Keep your money for yourself, Nikos. I don't want it. You bought me lunch, and I'm having your free hospitality at the villa—but I won't let you pay for my clothes.'

She walked off.

He strode after her, taking her arm. 'I did not mean—' he began.

'Yes, you did.'

Her contradiction was flat. Spots of colour were in her cheeks, anger in her voice. For a moment they simply eyeballed each other, then Nikos lifted his hand away.

Was this more virtue signalling on her part, like insisting on having lunch at that cheap tourist place? Well, it was his turn to insist on something now—and he would tell her so.

'OK, so I did,' he conceded. 'But even if you won't let me buy your clothes, there is one thing I insist you let me do...' Calmly he helped himself to her carrier bags. 'I'll carry these for you,' he told her.

For a moment—just a moment—those angry spots of colour stayed in Alys's cheeks. Then they vanished. She gave a reluctant half-laugh.

It was all Nikos needed.

It was the first laugh, however reluctant, he'd got out of her yet. That had to be worth something.

He felt his mood improve. The moment of conflict had passed.

'Let's get a drink,' he said amiably. 'And, just to show my respect for you, I'll let you buy.'

Carrier bags swinging in either hand, he set off up the road, Alys beside him.

Somehow, it felt good.

CHAPTER TEN

ALYS GAZED ABOUT HER. The top of the narrow street had opened out into the town's central square—'The *agora*…the old marketplace,' Nikos had informed her—which was dominated by a handsome church with the characteristic Orthodox dome.

There were several cafés at the edge of the square and Alys let Nikos choose one, grateful to sit down under a shady awning in the afternoon heat.

Had it made a difference, she wondered, insisting to Nikos that she pay for her own clothes? She hadn't been keen on spending her scarce money, but she really did need to supplement her wardrobe at the villa—and anyway there would be summers in England too, where such light garments would be fine.

Nikos gave their order to the waitress, who glided off. Alys was not unaware of her lingering glance at Nikos as he pushed his sunglasses up on his head and stretched out his long legs. Other female eyes belonging to the café's customers were coming his way. She was well aware of that too.

For a second so brief she hardly noticed it she felt a pang of possessiveness go through her. Then, dismayed, she caught herself. She had no claim on Nikos—none whatsoever. Carrying his baby conferred upon her nothing of the sort.

One day he'll marry some posh female from his own world—someone as rich as he is, so he won't have to fret that she's only interested in his money.

She tried to conjure up a feeling of caustic cynicism at the thought, but instead only that illogical out-of-place pang came again. She looked away out over the *agora*, blinking at the sun, dazzling on the white walls of the church...

Their drinks arrived—orange juice for herself, and a very Greek dark, thick black coffee for Nikos, together with iced water. They drank companionably enough, with Alys mostly peoplewatching, taking in the scene. She asked Nikos a few questions about the church and he answered what he knew, looking up more information on his phone for her, telling her which saint it was dedicated to and when it had been built.

'I know almost nothing about the Greek Orthodox Church,' Alys heard herself musing. 'The priests have long beards and there are icons... And Easter is a different time to ours, mostly. I've never understood why.'

Nikos explained it to her, how the Orthodox

church used the the older Julian calendar and the Latin churches the newer Gregorian calendar. Alys still wasn't sure she understood fully, but as they finished their drinks Nikos said, 'Would you like to see inside the church?'

Alys nodded and they got up, with Alys digging in her purse for the euros she needed to cover the drinks and a tip. Nikos, true to his earlier promise to let her pay, made no attempt to override her, and she felt she had won a small victory.

But did it amount to anything at all? Preferring a cheap tourist restaurant to a flash marina one, paying for her own clothes and buying Nikos a coffee might not be enough to convince him she was not after the Drakis money...

But I've made it clear I don't want child maintenance, that I can cope now he's paid my debts.

He hadn't contested her, she realised. Did that mean he'd accepted that she had no intention of leeching off him?

She didn't know. All she knew was that being with him was getting easier, less constrained, and she was less endlessly wary. Her guard was lowering, her reserve dissipating. She could hold a normal conversation with him now—talk about innocuous things, as they were doing now.

Nikos was holding open the heavy church door for her and she stepped inside. It was cool and dimly lit, rich with the scent of incense. Candles were set before gilded icons, and rich Byzantine murals glowed like jewels.

In a low voice, Nikos explained what she was seeing as she gazed about her.

This will be as much my baby's heritage as the parish churches of England.

Her eyes went to the baptismal font. Would Nikos want their baby christened? Well, if he did, there were Greek Orthodox churches in the UK, she thought defiantly. Yet for all her defiance, she felt, in this centuries-old church, the weight of tradition to which her baby would be heir.

Do I have a right to keep him or her from that?

Her chin lifted. All she'd said to Nikos was that she didn't want his money—not that she didn't want him to have anything to do with their son or daughter… But if he did want to play a part, have some kind of access to their child, what form would that take?

Her eyes went to him. It was he who'd insisted they stop being strangers, accept they were going to be parents together. Yes, he'd treated her like dirt to start with, insulted her unforgivably in his initial assumptions about her, but if he was setting them aside now—as he did seem to be doing—then wasn't he right to have brought her here? So that they could slowly, carefully accustom themselves not just to each other, but to shared parenthood?

But how shared?

The memory of what he'd said to her at that nightmare dinner in Athens sounded in her head.

'No child of mine will be born a bastard.'

He had told her, dictated to her as if she were the lowest of the low, that he would marry her to legitimise their baby—however much he clearly loathed the idea. Loathed the fact that she was pregnant, landing him with an unwanted child by an unwanted woman.

But he doesn't look at me with loathing any longer...

She felt her emotions well and shift within her, disturbing her certainties, her own assumptions that Nikos would far rather she had *not* got pregnant from their brief single night together.

'Seen enough?' Nikos was asking her now, and she nodded again, letting him show her out of the church.

The heat of the afternoon hit her as they stepped back into the *agora*.

'What would you like to do now?' he asked solicitously.

A wave of tiredness swept over her, and a longing for air conditioning. 'Would you think me very feeble if I said I'd like to go back to the villa now?' she asked.

He slid his dark glasses over his eyes now they were in the bright sunshine again. 'Alys, believe me, you are the very last woman on earth I would describe as feeble,' he said.

His voice was dry, but there was a wry humour in it that made her glance at him uncertainly. She wished she could still see his eyes—then was glad she could not.

Without her realising what he was about to do, he slid her hand into his. 'Come on, let's get you back to the car,' he said, and the humour was still in his voice. 'And if you come over feeble let me know—I'll carry you there!' he finished lightly.

Her carrier bags swung from his other hand as he started to walk forward, taking a quieter street than the one they'd come up, leading her back down to the seafront.

She went with him meekly, letting him keep her hand, because it was quite nice to be able to lean some of her weight on him as they headed down the paved road, uneven in places, with cars parked on either side. Alys realised it was the street he'd parked the SUV in and saw it, still huge and gleaming and expensive-looking beside the other vehicles, but right now a welcome sight.

'In you go,' Nikos said, opening the passenger door for her, and hefting her inside, placing her carrier bags in the footwell, then closing the door and moving around to his side, swinging himself into his seat.

He gunned the engine, carefully extricating the vehicle from the tight space, and Alys sat back in relief as the air con got going.

Nikos glanced at her as they gained the road out

of town. 'Time for home,' he said. 'And maybe a cooling dip in the pool before drinks. Sound good?'

He cocked an enquiring eyebrow at her, a smile playing around his mouth.

Alys nodded. 'Yes,' she said. Because it did sound good.

Nikos was accelerating, his eyes on the road, and Alys let her own eyes linger on his profile. She was feeling things she should not feel.

But did, all the same.

Nikos relaxed back in his chair at the dinner table, idly twirling his wine glass in his hand, letting his eyes rest on the woman sitting opposite. Alys, her hair freshly washed after their dip in the pool, waving in delicate tendrils over her shoulders, was wearing one of her newly purchased outfits: the yellow gypsy-style skirt and the pretty flower-sprigged green top.

And with all the judgementalism in the world he could not condemn it. Cheap it might be, but her natural beauty was such that she could make any outfit look as if it had cost a million...

He took another leisurely mouthful of his wine, savouring the bouquet. 'This really is very good,' he observed, setting down the glass and resuming eating. The rich lamb was tender and succulent, and he ate with a will. The island air seemed to give him an extra appetite. Or something did...

His eyes went back to Alys, lingering on her. He

felt desire rise within him and let it do so. Soon, maybe, he would be able to indulge it. But not quite yet. She was much less guarded with him now, and their outing today had moved them forward significantly, but she was not ready for him yet. He had made one heavy miscalculation with her already—he could not risk another. Not when she was still so determined to return to England...

Her words over lunch, telling him she would be a single mother, rang in his head, unwelcome, showing him just how far he still had to go.

He took another mouthful of the wine to distract him. It was, as Spiros had promised him, standing up well to the rich lamb.

'I'm only sorry you can't share it with me,' he said to Alys now, watching her sip at her iced pomegranate juice. 'Spiros persuaded me to try it. It's local, and I suspect the grower is one of his relatives.' There was a wry glint in his eye. 'Spiros is probably hoping I might like it and decide to invest in the winery.'

'Will you?' Alys asked.

He shook his head. 'Probably not.'

She looked at him. 'Why not? You were saying on our drive this morning that the island could do with more inward investment, reducing reliance on tourism. So why not from you?'

'Something like an individual winery is too small-scale for Drakis,' he replied. 'And wine itself is a risky business. Too many uncertainties—the weather, the harvest, changing consumer tastes…'

As he spoke, he knew he was echoing his father's views. He went on echoing them.

'Drakis investments are all very carefully planned, Alys, and on a scale you are probably incapable of comprehending. Risk has to be extremely carefully managed and minimised. Contained. By whatever means necessary.'

His eyes rested on her. *By whatever means necessary indeed…* And not just with financial risk. With risk that was far more important to contain. He felt himself tense, shuttered his eyes. So much depended on what he was doing now, here at the villa…

And if I get it wrong…

No, he would not be getting it wrong! He would be getting it right—totally right. And every day she spent here with him was proving that.

But Alys was talking to him, replying to him, and he made himself pay attention.

'Well, you could risk a bit on a vineyard, couldn't you?' she was saying. 'Wouldn't it be peanuts for you? So why not?' There was an encouraging note in her voice. 'After all, Spiros does a superb job of running this place for you, and however well paid he is, why not do something for him in return? At the very least,' she finished, 'if you like the wine so much you could buy a shedload of it off his relative!'

Nikos gave a laugh. 'OK!' he said, and held up his hand in a yielding gesture. 'I'll buy a good few cases and then maybe I'll think about investing in his expansion plans.'

Alys smiled at him warmly. It was a warmth that made him glad he'd made the reply he had.

'You see,' she said, 'you can be something more than a ruthless rainmaker—or whatever it is people like you are called—pulling money-spinning deals out of thin air!'

He gave another laugh, but he knew it was edged this time.

'It's not quite thin air, Alys,' he said. 'There's a hell of a lot of work involved in every one of them. I don't get much time off.'

She frowned. 'That's so stupid,' she said. 'What's the point of all your money if you don't get time to enjoy it?'

'It doesn't make itself,' he answered. Again, he heard his father's voice in his head as he spoke. Always another deal to set up, to see through to completion, to collect the profits on. And then another...

The way to be a true Drakis...

'Making money is what I do,' he spelt out.

Proving myself a worthy son, despite the disaster of my birth in the first place.

'Haven't you got enough by now? How much more do you want?' he heard her persist.

He wished she wouldn't.

He reached for his wine, took a hefty mouthful. She was speaking again, and there was something different in her voice now.

'You're so incredibly privileged, Nikos,' she was saying. He saw her gesture with her hand, indicating their surroundings. 'This fabulous villa, your lavish lifestyle, never having to worry about mundane things like paying bills… So why not enjoy it?' She was looking at him now. 'You said that you couldn't remember when you were last here. That's so sad! Such a waste!'

She looked away, and in the soft light from the candles and the table lamp her expression seemed to change.

'None of us know how long we've got on this earth, Nikos. We have to make the most of what we have while we have it. Life can change in an instant…devastatingly—'

She broke off. Nikos looked at her. 'That sounds personal,' he said slowly.

She swallowed. He saw her hand go in that increasingly familiar gesture to just below her midriff. He thought she might be about to say something, but she only blinked, looking away, out over the night-dark vista. The chorus of cicadas sounded louder in his ears, the heady scent of jasmine catching his senses.

'Look, there's a crescent moon!' he heard Alys exclaim, pointing behind him. 'Just visible.'

He craned his neck. 'New tonight,' he observed.

'You should make a wish,' he added, looking back at her with a half-smile.

His gaze clashed with hers and for a moment, an instant, they held.

Then she dropped her eyes, shaking her head. 'Wishes are dangerous things, Nikos,' she said.

Her voice was low, and he could hear, once more, a note of constraint in it. She moved to pick up her knife and fork again, to resume eating, but he reached out his hand, touched her wrist. The briefest touch.

'Not always, Alys,' he said.

Her eyes flew to his, and for an instant that was not so brief, they held his.

He gave a slow, intimate smile. 'Sometimes,' he said, and his eyes never let hers go for a moment, 'we do get what we wish for. And everything comes right.' His smile deepened, his eyes still holding hers. 'Everything...'

Alys stared at her reflection in the mirror behind the vanity unit in her en suite bathroom. She should get undressed, brush her teeth, go to bed, get a good night's sleep. But she could not. Her eyes were wide, and huge, gazing at herself. In her head, those words of Nikos's at dinner played like a refrain she could not unhear. Did not want to unhear.

'Sometimes we do get what we wish for. And everything comes right. Everything...'

She felt her breath catch in her throat.

What's happening to me?

Her reflected gaze stared back at her, giving her no answer. But she did not need one. She knew what was happening to her.

But I can't let it. We had one night together, that's all—one single night, nothing more.

Her expression changed.

But he came back to find you—he did want more!

She pressed her hands down on the surface of the vanity unit, whitening the tips of her fingers with the pressure of it.

OK, so we might have had an affair—but that would have been all! Nothing to keep us together.

Yet again her expression changed.

But now there is something to keep us together. A baby that links us for ever…

She gave a low cry in her throat and turned away, hearing her own voice again now in her head.

'Wishes are dangerous things, Nikos.'

She went back into her bedroom. The luxury of it was familiar to her now. So was being waited on hand and foot by Spiros and his staff, not having to lift a finger for herself. Nikos all solicitude towards her…

Nikos was familiar to her…

They'd been here only a handful of days, and yet she knew that all the wariness she'd arrived with was all but gone already. He was so unutterably different now from the way he had been in Athens it was almost impossible to think he had ever spoken to her so hideously, treated her so contemptuously, made such ugly, harsh assumptions about her, such accusations…

It's like it never was. Like the way it was when we met the way we did. Drawn together…unable to resist each other.

With another cry stifled in her throat, she paced restlessly around the room. Then she halted, remembering more of what Nikos had said that evening. Talking of risk. For him, it was business risk. But for her—

Her expression grew troubled.

He talked about minimising risk, containing it. And isn't that what I have to do too? Isn't that why I don't want him looking at me the way he does sometimes? Why I don't want him taking my hand, or lifting me out of a boat or—?

She resumed her pacing, as if it could bring release from her tormenting thoughts. But that, she found, was not possible.

Nor was it possible the following day.

Seeing Nikos at breakfast seemed harder than before, yet for a completely different reason. Did a slight colour run up her cheeks as she took her place, wearing one of her new tee shirts and the new blue shorts, knowing that the expression in his eyes was telling her he was liking what he was seeing.

'So, what kind of day would you like today?' Nikos was asking, his tone genial. 'Another outing, or something more lazy?'

Alys poured herself some orange juice—freshly squeezed, she knew, not from a carton. It tasted delicious, and she also knew, with an inner sigh, that she was getting used to all this luxury. Dangerously used to it...

'Could we do lazy?' she asked.

'Of course we could,' Nikos said. 'Breakfast, pool, lunch, beach, drinks, dinner. Sound OK?'

She made a wry face. 'How could it not?' she answered. She looked about her and gave a sigh.

'Why the sigh?'

Was there concern in his voice? She looked back at him. 'Because this is all just so beautiful,' she said, putting her thoughts into words. She looked at him across the table. 'I meant what I said last night, you know. You should make the very most of having a place like this.' She gave him a humorous smile. 'Promise me you'll come here every summer from now on. For at least a fortnight! Take time off from work—force yourself to have a holiday!'

He gave a laugh, and it tugged at a memory of how his laugh had been so ready that first dinner they'd shared together in London.

Are we getting like that again, little by little?

She pulled back mentally. She must not wish for what it was dangerous to wish for…

But it was hard not to. Increasingly hard.

The lazy day passed just as she had asked—with extreme leisure. Down at the poolside she opened one of the English language books she'd found, as Nikos had said, on the bookshelf in the beautifully appointed lounge, with its picture windows opening to the terrace. It was, of all things, Jane Austen's *Emma*, and she found herself happily absorbed in the familiar tale.

Nikos seemed to have finished his original action adventure paperback, and was now on to a legal drama, full of corrupt politicians and twists and turns of plot. He had no idea yet how they would turn out, he informed her as they compared reading matter.

'I can't remember how many times I've read *Emma*,' she mused. 'That's the joy of Austen— something new every time, and what's familiar so delightful anyway. And every time I read a new lit crit of any of her novels there's something fresh to discover.'

He looked across at her from his lounger. '"Lit crit"? That sounds quite heavy duty.'

'I did English Literature at university,' she answered. She swallowed. 'I never finished, though.'

'You dropped out?' Was there disapproval in his voice.

'Yes,' she said. 'Just before Finals. Maybe one day... Well, perhaps I can repeat my third year, claw back a degree. It would help, I know, when it comes to getting a better paid job.'

He was still looking at her, a frown on his face. 'Why did you drop out?'

She didn't want to talk about it. Wished she'd never mentioned it. 'Life changed,' she said shortly.

She turned a page, making it obvious she was reading. She was conscious of his head still turned towards her, but she would say no more. It was too raw. Too painful.

But Nikos was speaking again. 'Is that when you ran up those debts?' he asked, and there was an edge in his voice now.

She did not look at him. 'Yes,' she said. 'Things got...difficult.'

'Were you living it up in London? Spending more than you could afford? It's easy to do if you hang out with the wrong people in the wrong places...places they can afford, but you can't...'

He paused, and she knew he was still looking at her.

'Like the party I met you at.'

She set down *Emma* and looked across at him, stung by the implicit accusation he was making. Her voice was flat as she riposted, 'I was only at that party because I was spending the weekend with an old uni friend who lives in London and whose flatmate works in the fashion industry. She wangled us all an invite to that flash bash that night. My friend lent me a dress—a size too small for me, as I'm sure you could tell pretty instantly. I didn't like the party the minute I got there, and I was about to cut and run when—' She broke off. 'You know the rest. You were there.'

'Yes,' he acknowledged, and now that edge was no longer in his voice. 'And I was about to "cut and run" as well—I only turned up because I knew the guy hosting it through a business contact and I wanted to catch him about something. He proved elusive, so I was about to leave myself. Until…' He gave a half-laugh. 'Well, you know the rest too.' He paused. 'And now here we are…' he said slowly.

'Yes,' she said, and swallowed.

She picked up *Emma* again, immersing herself so she didn't have to think about all the complications in her life. Only one thing in it was simple. Her free hand went to her abdomen, curving around it. Whatever happened—whatever it turned out to be, this messy, difficult, complicated situation with Nikos—her baby, she vowed, would be safe.

Whatever I have to do.

Nikos lay back in the warm pool water, floating buoyantly in the ultimate form of relaxation. Alys was still reading *Emma*, lying back on her lounger.

His thoughts played through his head. There were contradictions in what she'd just told him. She'd been to university, yet dropped out. Run up debts, yet not from a hard-partying lifestyle, so she claimed. Yesterday she'd said she didn't want any maintenance from him for the baby, talked about being a working mother, refused to let him pay for those cheap clothes she'd bought. So…virtue signalling to impress him, or genuinely meant?

He gave a mental shrug. Did it matter? It wasn't going to alter what was going to happen. His plans for her were not derailable.

And yet…

I don't want her to be what I don't want her to be.

It was a convoluted thought, but it made sense to him.

I'm glad that when I took her to bed she was the way she was. Glad that I couldn't get that night out of my head—glad that I wanted to go back to find her…claim her again.

His thoughts flickered in his head like that faulty electrical circuit again, trying to make the connections that would let the current flow smoothly, powerfully.

And when she went into that meltdown at the airport…maybe I was glad of that too.

He frowned. Glad that she had wanted to bolt back to England?

Glad of why she wanted to—because she felt

I'd accused her unfairly, made assumptions about why she'd got in touch with me, about what she wanted from me.

And he was going on being glad. For many, many reasons.

Glad that she's now warming to me, that I'm winning her round. Glad, too, even if it was just virtue signalling, that she didn't want me to buy her clothes or take her shopping at the marina.

He opened his eyes, turning his head in the water towards where she was lying, one hand still curved protectively where her baby lay beneath.

Glad, above all, for that...

His eyes lingered on her, moved up to her face. Her eyes were moving as she read, tender lips slightly parted, the warm flush of heat on her cheeks, the honeying tan of the sun on her skin.

Despite the cool water he felt arousal stir.

With a contraction of his abs he flipped over, diving down to the bottom of the pool. Cooling his ardour.

At least for now.

CHAPTER ELEVEN

'WE'VE HAD TWO lazy days in a row,' Nikos announced, glancing across the breakfast table at Alys, 'so today it's out and about. Tell me—how's your head for heights?'

She looked at him cautiously. 'No abseiling down from the radio tower on the top of that mountain,' she adjured him.

He gave a laugh. 'Nothing like that,' he promised.

She was intrigued, but he would not be drawn.

She found out soon enough—after breakfast. Nikos led her up the staircase to the villa's front door, stepped out. Alys looked around. No car had been parked up for them, and the area was deserted.

'What—?' she began, but Nikos put a finger against her lips.

'Listen,' he said.

And then she heard it. The staccato stutter of a helicopter approaching.

A moment later it was soaring over the cypress trees encircling the wide gravelled area, sending the branches into a frenzy of whipping as it hovered a moment and then swooped down to land. The noise was deafening, even when the pilot cut the engine to idle.

Nikos took her hand. 'Come on!' he shouted. 'And duck when I do!'

She did, and he ran forward with her, lifting her inside as the pilot opened the passenger door for them. She took her seat, Nikos beside her, but still couldn't hear a thing until he handed her a pair of headphones, donning another pair himself.

Instantly he was audible and the noisy engine was not. 'Fancy a bird's-eye view of the island?' he asked, and grinned.

The pilot lifted off, and Alys gave a gasp as they crowned the trees, seeing the villa drop away below as the helicopter gyred around, heading out to sea.

It was incredible, it was amazing, and Alys loved every single moment of it. They circled the island, dipping sometimes almost to wave level, churning up the surface of the sea, then soared upwards again, heading inland to skim the peaks of the rocky interior before speeding out to sea again. Alys stared, enchanted, as far below sailing craft and motorboats and the ferry to the neighbouring islands were turned to miniature toys.

Eventually they had seen everything, and Nikos instructed the pilot to take them down. But they did not land at the villa. They were lowered down onto a helipad by the marina, a massive 'H' denoting just where the chopper should deposit them.

As he helped her out, guiding her to the edge of the helipad as the pilot took off again, Alys turned to him. Her eyes were shining.

'That was *fabulous*, Nikos! Thank you!'

He gave a laugh, clearly pleased with her open delight. 'We'll go back home the same way,' he promised her. 'But first…'

He was looking at her with a glint in his eye. Was it a challenge? She wasn't quite sure. But when he spoke she became sure.

'Now it's time for part two of today's mystery treat,' he announced. 'And, Alys, please…' the glint wasn't in his eye now, he wore a different expression, more serious '…accept this from me.'

She looked at him uncertainly. 'Accept what?' she asked.

He didn't answer immediately, but walked her away from the helipad, down to where the marina proper opened up. An array of sleek, expensive-looking boats were moored in a neat line on one side of the wide concourse, and on the other side an array of equally sleek, expensive-looking restaurants and shops. He headed for one of them, and Alys realised it was a beauty salon.

'A pampering session,' he told her. 'To counter some of the sun and sea's wear and tear on you.

It's very popular, so I'm told, for yachties when they dock.'

Mixed feelings filled Alys. She wanted to refuse to let Nikos spend what she knew perfectly well would be a hefty sum of money on her, for whatever treatments an obviously upmarket place like this offered its wealthy clients. But there was something in his expression that stayed her.

'Please,' he said. 'It's for you.'

Her expression flickered. Then, 'Thank you,' she said.

She didn't say more than that. There seemed to be a bit of a lump in her throat, and she blinked.

Then Nikos was taking her elbow, guiding her into the salon before she had a chance to change her mind and object.

Inside, the receptionist greeted them fulsomely, her smile encompassing them both. But Alys did not fail to recognise that she was being especially fulsome towards Nikos.

Because he's clearly Mr Rich? Or because he's making her knees turn to jelly by being probably the most fantastic-looking bloke she's set eyes on in her life?

She didn't have time to come up with an answer—it was probably both anyway—before two members of staff appeared from the back of the reception area and whisked her away.

There then followed nearly two hours of what most definitely deserved the description 'pampering'. She was given a body wrap, a face peel, a pedicure and a massage. And then, having showered and had a gown swathed about her, she was ushered into the hair salon section, where she had her hair done while her nails were manicured and lightly lacquered in clear varnish.

Finally she was shown back to the changing room, where the final touch of Nikos's lavish treat was waiting for her.

'Mr Drakis has had these delivered from the boutique next door,' she was informed brightly.

Alys stared at the dresses hanging from the rail. All three were beautiful. Floaty-looking sundresses in floral patterns in different hues. For a moment she stilled, her memory going back to how Nikos had had that beautiful designer cocktail dress delivered to her hotel room the night of that nightmare dinner in Athens.

Emotion knifed in her and she almost turned to the assistant to demand her own clothes back—the cheap shorts and tee shirt she'd bought herself. Then she took a breath. This wasn't a repeat of that dress in Athens.

We've moved on since then—things are better between us now.

That was what she had to believe—because it was true.

Slowly, she breathed out, turned to the assistant. 'Thank you,' she said.

The young woman smiled brightly. 'There is

lingerie to go with them, and a choice of shoes. When you are ready, we will do your make-up.'

She smiled again, and whisked out of the room.

Nikos sat in the reception area, long legs stretched out as he leafed through a motoring magazine he'd brought with him from the premises next door. There was a sound from the rear of the area and he looked up. Alys was emerging.

Every muscle in his body clenched—and then slowly...infinitely slowly...relaxed.

Thee mou, she looked...

Breathtaking, enchanting, gorgeous, fabulous, fantastic...and just enchantingly beautiful!

All the dresses he'd chosen after she'd disappeared into the salon were exactly right. The sales assistant had helped him. But of the three he'd selected, the one she was wearing was his favourite. It was white, in ultra-fine cotton, with a print of delicate pale blue flowers across the bodice, deepening to a richer blue on the softly gathered calf-length skirt that showed off to perfection the turn of her slender ankles, themselves enhanced by the low-heeled, strappy sandals that exposed the elegant arch of her foot.

As for the rest of her...

Her hair had been washed and styled, trimmed a little, then blow-dried into a sleek, smooth fall over her shoulders, waving back from her face. Another wash of appreciation went through him.

A face that had been subtly made up to give her already lightly tanned skin a peachy glow, with a little shadow to deepen her eyes, a touch of mascara to darken her lashes, a light lipstick to give her lips a sheen.

He got to his feet, his magazine tossed aside, and moved towards her, hands outstretched. 'You look…' he breathed '…absolutely wonderful!'

His eyes worked over her again, showing in their open gaze all his appreciation of what he was seeing.

A slight colour washed up her cheeks. 'Yes,' she said dryly, 'it's amazing what a very expensive round of pampering can do. And a very expensive frock.'

He shook his head. 'They need the base material to work on,' he told her. 'And you…' He took a breath. 'You have it in abundance.'

He lifted his hand to encompass the staff present.

'Ladies, thank you! You've made me a happy, happy man!' His smile was broad, his thanks to them well deserved. Then he turned back to Alys. 'Time for lunch,' he said.

He led the way out—he'd settled the bill already, not even glancing at it—and they emerged into the hot sun. He could feel his stomach growl, and hunger bite.

And not just for food.

But he set that other hunger aside. Time for that later...

For now... 'It's just along here,' he told Alys.

There were several restaurants to choose from, but he'd chosen the one with the best view of the marina. He wondered whether Alys was going to demur, or say she'd rather eat at one of the harbour-side tavernas. But it seemed, since she had acquiesced gracefully to the pampering session, and the outfits he'd bought her, that she was going to do likewise now about lunching here at the marina.

He was appreciative of all the concessions on her part. His eyes went to her again as they took their seats. He was appreciative of so, so much...

She was studying her menu. 'Definitely *not* tourist fare,' she remarked dryly, but with a touch of humour.

Food orders taken—calamari for him, grilled fish for Alys, with a light starter of a courgette terrine for both of them—he sat back to taste his chilled Chablis as Alys sipped from her gently fizzing elderflower spritzer.

'So what did you do, Nikos, while I was being pampered to within an inch of my life?' Alys asked. 'Besides going shopping for expensive frocks for me?'

'Next door to the salon is a gym and a barber shop. I indulged in both. Cycled ten kilometres... did some weights—then got a massage and,' he added, smoothing an appreciative hand over his ultra-smooth jaw, 'the ultimate male indulgence: a professional cut-throat wet shave! Nothing to beat it. Oh, and the barber trimmed my hair as well—haven't you noticed?'

He cast a smiling challenging look at Alys, and saw colour run up her cheeks again.

'Yes, I did, actually,' she answered. 'You look very smart, Nikos,' she said, with deliberate approval.

Her eyes met his, and for all the note of humour in her voice she dropped her gaze again, colour still in her cheeks.

Satisfaction flowed through Nikos and his state of relaxation increased. This was good…this was *all* good.

And it went on being good.

The food was excellent—even if it was not, he mused with good-humoured irony, as hearty as the tourist fare at the taverna—his wine was excellent and his company for lunch was excellent. Not just to look at, breathtaking though it was every time his eyes went to Alys, but to enjoy in conversation. Conversation that was, as he was not slow to appreciate, as easy now as it had been in London, over dinner together that first night.

That only night.

And now it's back. Back for good.

He would permit no other possibility.

As they finally left the restaurant, strolling out onto the marina concourse, Nikos's eyes went to her figure. The breeze moulded the soft fabric of her frock to her body, and the contours of her full figure were clearly noticeable to him.

For a moment, while his eyes rested on the gentle swell exposed by the tautened fabric, his expression shadowed. Whatever Alys might proclaim or prefer, there was going to be only one outcome he would permit. And he would make very, very sure she wanted it too…

Alys stood half leaning on the balustrade edging the terrace beyond the dining table, where there was less light to occlude the stars and the newly risen moon, its crescent thicker now.

Her mood was strange. She was exquisitely conscious of Nikos standing next to her, though scrupulously not too close. For all that, she could still feel him close to her, and was aware of how she looked to him.

She was still wearing the dress he'd bought for her, now with the little lacy bolero—cashmere, she fancied wryly—that had been lying wrapped in tissue paper on the seat of the helicopter, along with her own clothes, when they'd finally emerged from the long and leisurely lunch that had gone on into mid-afternoon.

The flight back to the villa had been less swooping than the one in the morning, instead taking them along a valley leading into the interior, where they had hovered over a Mycenaean-era archaeological site that was yet to be fully excavated, and so was best seen from the air.

Alys had been fascinated, listening to Nikos telling her what he had read up on it. Then they had headed back to the villa in time for Alys to freshen up before emerging onto the terrace for drinks and then dinner. She'd put her hair up into a loose chignon and touched up her make-up, knowing, with a tiny tremor of her hand as she carefully reapplied her mascara, just why she was doing so.

She had known it again as, seated opposite him across the dining table on the terrace, he'd raised his glass to her, the ruby wine winking in the candlelight as he'd murmured his tribute.

'To a perfect day,' he'd said. And then something in his voice had changed, deepened. 'And to your perfect beauty.'

She had accepted the tribute, no longer rejecting it. Something had run between them...something that she had necessarily held at bay, scarred as she was by his harsh, contemptuous condemnation of her.

But that was all gone now—as if it had never been. And if it was no longer there, then...

Then I do not have to hold him at bay, do not have to hold myself at bay, nor tell myself that I must not, should not...

Instead...

Instead she had done as she had been doing all day, and over dinner she had let her gaze mingle with his, let his gaze wash over her, telling her just what he had told her that very first night together... how much he desired her...

Like it was that very first evening.

Back then, she had given herself up with wonder and delight to what had happened between them.

But it was simple then. Desire was a flame burning between us, unable to be quenched, unwilling to be extinguished, for there was no reason to do so.

But now? Now it was not simple at all...

As she leant against the still-warm balustrade she felt her hand drop to where her tiny baby was growing, day by day. Complicating everything. Demanding, requiring, deserving only the best, the *very* best, for its little life...

Had Nikos seen her gesture? She did not know.

But a finger lifted to her cheek, drawing slowly down it. Eyes dipping to hers. 'Beautiful Alys...' he murmured.

That huskiness was in his voice, as it had been when he had toasted her beauty. His eyes held hers, and she was helpless to free herself.

'You do know...' he spoke again, his voice still husky '...that this has been waiting for us. This moment now. Nothing has changed that. Nothing can ever change it. From the first I have desired you...and I desire you still.' He took a slow breath, his eyes drowning hers. 'I always shall.' Something changed in his eyes—something infinitesimal. 'And now that you carry my child...'

She gazed up at him, feeling the line where his touch had been. She could feel her pulse start to beat faster, feel the breathlessness inside her.

'Nikos, I...'

There was a question in her voice, her eyes. She stepped away. The sliding doors into her bedroom were behind her, and she moved to slip them open. But her hand was caught by his, staying her.

'Alys...'

He said her name again—softly, sensually—and the huskiness accentuated his accent, sending weakness through her. She turned back, and he was dark against the night sky.

'Don't hold me away,' he said, his voice low. 'Not any longer. Not tonight...'

And then he was stepping towards her, past her, sliding open the glass door, drawing her within. Drawing her to him. Into his arms.

And now she could question no longer—could only know what had always been between them, only do what she had day by day been yielding to, deny it all she could, resist it all she would...

She could do so no longer. And as his mouth lowered to hers, easing her lips open to his, his hands at her spine, making her pliant towards him, she gave a little sigh, her body folding to his, yielding to his...

It was bliss, it was wonder, and it was all the

sweet, sensual pleasure that had ever been between them. He was teasing and tasting the honey of her mouth, opening it to his. Her hand was stealing to the strong column of his neck, moving around his muscled waist, and she was feeling, with a little shock as her hips pressed to his, just how powerfully his body was reacting to hers...

A moan broke from her and he drew back, holding her in the circle of his arms, gazing down at her. In his eyes desire blazed and burned.

'You do not know,' he said, 'how I have craved this moment.'

His eyes held hers and she could feel hers distending, feel the brand of his hands on her spine, holding her body to him, feel his desire for her. She could feel the blood surging in her veins, heat filling her as, his eyes never relinquishing their hold on hers, one of his hands dropped from her spine, came around her body and closed, slowly and possessively, over her breast.

It flowered beneath his touch, cresting and filling, and she gave another low, helpless moan as pleasure—oh, such sweet, honeyed pleasure—swirled within her. Her legs seemed to weaken, and she could feel his body harden against hers more powerfully yet.

Then he was kissing her again, his hand still cupping her breast, palming its crested peak. His other hand was moving up her spine—gliding, she realised dimly, inchoately, with one smooth movement the zip to her dress down. He eased it from her shoulders, never letting go her mouth, until the soft fabric fell to the ground, pooling at her feet.

For a moment he stood away from her, and she could only stand there with the lacy bra, the wisp of her panties all that shielded her nakedness from him. She felt her heart thudding in her chest, drumming in her ears.

His eyelids swept down. He was fastening his gaze on the swell of her abdomen. 'Like a sweetly ripening peach…'

His voice was low and he stepped towards her, one hand reaching to splay across her softly rounded body. Something moved in his eyes, and then he was sweeping her up into his arms, striding to the waiting bed, laying her down upon it.

To make her his again.

Completely his.

Only in the moment before his possession, as her body throbbed with her own desire, did he pause, gaze down at her, his face stark.

'I… I would not hurt you,' he said. 'Or—'

His hand splayed over her abdomen as protectively as the gesture she made herself. She felt her heart swell.

She lifted her head, raising her mouth to his, brushing it softly. 'You never could, Nikos,' she told him. 'Not now.'

For a moment their eyes held, and for a second

she thought she saw his veil. Then it was gone, as if it were impossible it should ever have been.

Her hands came around his back, lightly resting there. Then slowly, deliberately, never letting go his eyes, she pulled him down to her. Yielding to him completely. And to her own desire.

And to so much more...

CHAPTER TWELVE

Dim light was dissolving the darkness of the night away. Her bedroom drapes undrawn, Alys lay in the circle of Nikos's arms, strong and warm around her. Sleep still meshed her, and her rousing to wakefulness was only temporary...enough only to let emotion fill her. Certainty possess her.

Her arms tightened around Nikos's waist as if she would never let him go.

And I never will. Not now!

The same emotion swept through her again, wondrous in its realisation, bringing a smile to the lips pressed against his chest, secret and blissful. Then drowsiness took her again and she felt the sweet ache of her body, her thighs mingling with his, the soft swell of where, secretly within, their baby nestled safely.

The smile stayed on her lips as she gave herself to sleep once more.

Safe in Nikos's arms...

Safe for ever...

Nikos was making a hearty breakfast. He needed it. He deserved it.

A sense of supreme accomplishment filled him

from head to foot. Satisfaction in every cell in his body. Satisfaction on every count.

Mentally, as he reached for another fresh bread roll, generously slathering it with butter and honey, he ran through the reasons for his extraordinarily good mood on this bright, sun-drenched morning, with the Aegean sea girdling his vision, cicadas merrily striating away in the lush vegetation, the bougainvillea, vivid and vibrant, the honeysuckle and jasmine cascading all around, scenting the air with their rich fragrance, mingling with the aroma of freshly brewed coffee.

His reasons were not hard to find. And they all focussed on the woman sitting opposite him, gracefully pouring orange juice.

He felt emotion clench inside him. So much emotion. Relief, pure and unadulterated, that finally he could set aside all that had beset him from the moment his eyes had scanned that letter left for him at the concierge's desk in London, that had plunged him into a darkness he had been fighting to emerge from ever since.

And now he was clear of it! Completely and totally clear! Everything had come right.

His gaze went to her, the woman who would now never again threaten to bolt back to England, who would never hold any kind of malign power over him, would never oppose him again or resist him again…

Because now, finally, she had no more reason to want to do so. No reason at all.

She is mine completely now.

Alys lolled lazily, half in the warm shallow water lapping at her, half on the soft sand, as Nikos, emerging from his vigorous swim, hunkered down beside her to kiss her with a salty mouth.

'You taste of the sea.' She laughed.

'And you taste of honey,' he replied, kissing her again, then rolling back beside her, taking his weight, as she was doing, on his elbows.

'Glad we came back here?' he asked.

'Oh, yes!' she agreed warmly.

They had taken the motorboat out again, to the secret cove at the tip of the promontory. But this time how much more wonderful it was! She felt a glow go through her, emotions turning over and over inside her.

Nikos kissed her again, more lingeringly this time.

'You do realise, don't you, why I've brought you here?' he said, his expression revealing. 'Because there is absolutely no way this place can be overlooked. Which means...' his voice deepened '... that after lunch I intend to make mad, passionate love to you right here on the beach.' A wicked look entered his eyes, making Alys quiver with delight. 'I might even carry you off into the sea and make love to you all over again.'

Her eyes danced. 'Is it possible?' she asked. 'In the sea?'

The wicked look intensified. 'You'll just have to wait and find out,' he said, and kissed her again.

His kiss deepened but Alys drew back, a wicked look in her own eyes now.

'You said *after* lunch, Nikos! And don't you need to ensure you have enough energy for mad, passionate lovemaking?' she teased.

'True,' he allowed, and levered himself to his feet, drawing her up with him.

Her hand held his tightly. Was it really only so short a time ago when she had hesitated to let him do so? Hesitated to let there be any kind of physical contact with him, however mild or brief.

Because it was just too risky...

She felt the same emotion that had filled her when Nikos had kissed her flow through her again. The emotion that was always there now, like the warm, bright glow of the sun.

How unnecessary her fears had been! There had been no risk at all—none! All risk had vanished away, burnt off by the hot passion of Nikos's searing embraces. Making everything all right between them.

Because how could it not be right? Nikos had made it right! In his arms, safe and cherished, it was all so obvious to her now.

I'm in love with him! Totally, completely in love! Impossible to fight it, deny it, or fear it...

For there was nothing more to fight, or deny, or fear...

I love him—I carry his child—and we shall make our future together.

How could it be otherwise? Hadn't he declared that evening in Athens, when it had all gone so hideously wrong between them, that they must marry? Then, the way he'd said it, the way he'd thought of her, had only repelled and repulsed her, sending her fleeing. But now everything was different.

Now I want to marry him—can think of nothing that I long for more...loving him as I do...

She felt her heart turn over inside her, swelling and filling her with joy and wonder and delight. She laced her fingers in his, loving the feel of them, loving him beside her as they walked up the beach to where they'd set up camp, just as last time, under the shade of a sheltering rock.

As before, the kitchen at the villa had done them proud, and the wicker hamper was groaning with picnic treats. And after they'd eaten, just as he'd promised her he would, Nikos made love to her slowly, leisurely, taking his time, bringing her to a throbbing climax that made her cry out, unguarded in this remote, deserted spot, as her body convulsed around his, fusing with him in a shared pleasure so intense her hands clenched over his shoulders, her neck arching, as she cried out again when he surged within her.

Then later, strength restored, he made good on

his second promise—hefting her gloriously naked, as was he, into his arms, and striding laughingly out into the sea. Where, Alys discovered, to her amazement and delight and intense, thrilling pleasure, that, yes, making love while cradled by the water's buoyant swell was indeed perfectly, blissfully possible.

As was making love in the shower of her en suite bathroom on their return to the villa…and before and after breakfast…and in the pool house…and in Nikos's own bed all night long in the blissful, passionate days that followed.

Day after day after day.

Night after night.

In a happiness so perfect that time stopped completely…

And yet…

She stood beside him now, languorous after dinner, leaning on the balustrade, lazily looking out into the warm night, watching the moon rise in the night sky. It had waxed to full, and waned to dark, and was now once again a new silvered crescent against the stars.

She might not feel the time passing, but it was all the same. Her body was telling her so—not just the cycle of the moon. Her pregnancy was advancing inexorably, her body was filling out, her baby growing within.

How long will we stay here?

Nikos had said nothing about leaving the villa,

the island, nothing at all about what would happen when they did, as surely they must at some point? He had said nothing, she realised with a little frown, of their future at all. Like herself, he seemed content only to continue this lotus-eating lifestyle, with day merging into day, night into night, blissfully easy and idle, indulgent and lazy.

She wanted to ask him, yet also did not want to. Wanted to continue as they were, idle and leisured in this peaceful, beautiful place that had brought her her life's happiness.

And his?

She looked at him now, at his so familiar profile, feeling the little rush of love that always overcame her when she gazed at him.

I love him—but does he love me?

It was a question she did not want to ask, and even as she thought it she dismissed it. The way he was with her was enough for her—how could it not be? The Nikos who had been so coldly critical, hostile and contemptuous of her, laying down his diktats and demands, had gone completely. Here, at this beautiful villa, he'd become once more the man who had melted her like honey from the very first, with the heat of desire in his dark eyes... And now he was so much more than that.

A man so very dear to her.

A man I want to live my life with—make a family with.

And surely he must want that too! For why else

would he have swept her into his arms, his bed, as he had?

She felt her heart turn over again as she lifted his hand from where it lay on the stone balustrade, pressing it against her mouth and then her cheek.

He turned to smile down at her. Was it the moonlight, the starlight, or the candlelight from the dinner table that made her think she saw something move in his eyes? She could not tell what it was and then it was gone. Replaced by a very, very familiar look.

'Enough moon-gazing,' he told her.

His dark eyes glinted in the way that always—every time—made her weak at the knees.

'Time for bed—'

He lowered his hand, keeping hers within his, to lead her indoors. And willingly...oh, so willingly... Alys went with him.

Nikos opened the door of the office suite that the villa housed and reluctantly stepped inside, conscious that Andreas and the maids would be setting out breakfast and that he'd left Alys getting dressed after their morning lovemaking.

He did not want to do this.

But I can't avoid it any longer.

He could not go on holding the world at bay, however much he longed to.

Steeling himself, he stepped inside, closed the

door behind him, and settled himself down at the desk.

He turned on the computer. Sent the message he needed to send, that he could put off no longer...

'I have to go back to Athens.'

The words fell from Nikos as Alys looked at him across the breakfast table. She searched his face, hoping that the dismay his out-of-the-blue words had engendered in her was not showing in her own.

She tried to keep her tone nothing more than enquiring as she replied. 'Do...do I go too?'

'No, you can stay here for now. It won't take long...what I have to do in Athens.'

His words should have been reassuring, yet their effect on her was the opposite. She looked at him, with a troubled, questioning look in her eyes. Yet why should that be? She knew they could not stay here at the villa, cut off from the world in this blissful lotus-eating idyll for ever—that at some point he, at least, a man of business affairs, with all the responsibilities that pressed upon him, responsibilities that he had neglected for her sake, must reclaim them again. And besides, she and Nikos had to make their own plans and preparations for the future.

Plans to marry—for surely that will be what we'll do? Marry and make a family together.

Yet he had never made any mention of such a

future for them—not since that nightmare night in Athens.

But everything is completely different now between us! Now, instead of the thought sending me fleeing, marrying him is all that I long for!

Another thought came to her, and she clung to it. Perhaps that was the reason for his sudden announcement that he must go to Athens. Perhaps it was to make the necessary arrangements for their marriage...

But then why not say so?

She felt unease pluck at her again, tried not to let it show in her voice. 'When do you leave?'

'Today. After breakfast. That will give me more time in Athens.' He made no mention of when he would return, only going on to say, 'You'll be fine here. Spiros will look after you, so just take it easy, OK?'

She gave a smile, forcing her voice to sound relaxed. 'It's impossible to do anything else here, Nikos!'

He laughed, and the familiar sound was reassuring, diluting her unease. But when, after they had breakfasted, she went with him to the SUV parked above the villa, her questioning unease returned in strength. Nikos had an air about him that was abstracted, preoccupied. Tense.

When will I see him again?

The question echoed in her head as she accompanied him to the car. Spiros was at the wheel, for he would bring the vehicle back from the airport.

Nikos turned to her, taking her face in his hands, lifting it to his. There was something in his face, his eyes, she had never seen before, and it troubled her. For a moment she thought he was going to speak, but then, with a dipping of his long lashes, he simply dropped a swift, fleeting kiss on her mouth and released her, climbing into the SUV.

Spiros gunned the engine and set off. She raised a hand as the vehicle left the gravelled forecourt.

But whether Nikos returned her salute or not she did not know. Her eyes were tearing up and she could not see.

She turned away, going back indoors. Feeling desolate.

And unaccountably, out of nowhere, fearful.

Athens was hot, crowded, oppressive. Sultry with heat as if a storm must break. Nikos's expression was grim as the airport taxi dropped him off at the opulent Drakis mansion in the exclusive suburb of Kifissia.

I have a storm of my own ready to break over me.

And break it did.

His father's rage was incandescent, as Nikos had known it would be. He let it pour over him as he stood in his father's study like a recalcitrant schoolboy, but he had come to know his father well enough over the years to know that until his temper was spent there would be no rational conversation possible.

So he simply stood there, stonily, while his father raged about his utter irresponsibility in disappearing as he had, abrogating all his duties, endangering half a dozen essential half-completed deals and abandoning delicate negotiations with parties both in Europe and the USA. Costing a fortune in lost business!

'So where the *hell* have you been? You just disappeared without trace—your imbecile of a PA had no idea! Only said you were not answering your phone or replying to messages! Outrageous! Absolutely outrageous!'

'I've been at the villa.' Nikos cut across his father, his voice as tight as a drawn bowstring.

Colour mounted dangerously in his father's face, and he looked ready to explode again, but Nikos leant forward, placing his hands flat on his father's desk.

'I have something to tell you. Something vitally important to me. And...' he took a deep breath '... something to ask of you.'

Alys was lying by the pool, the afternoon sun warm on her bare back, but uneasiness still filled her—as it had since she had bade Nikos farewell that morning. She tried to make herself relax, but it was impossible. Then, above the constant chorus of the cicadas all about in the vegetation around the pool deck, she heard a new noise.

Rhythmic, heavy. Getting closer.

She twisted her head, staring into the cerulean sky. It was a helicopter, approaching over the sea from the west. She levered herself up, watching it grow closer, distinctly heading towards the villa.

She felt her heart leap. Nikos—coming back already!

She pulled her tee shirt and shorts on over her swimsuit, gathered her things, hurrying as best she could up the steep steps to the top terrace, hearing the helicopter make its descent to the forecourt. She wanted to be there to greet Nikos when he landed.

But as she finally gained the terrace, breathless, Spiros was hurrying forward out of the villa, his manner agitated, his customary cheerfulness quite absent.

Alarm filled her. 'Spiros, what is it? Has something happened?'

He beckoned her indoors. 'You must come,' he told her. 'At once!'

Nikos took his seat in the New York–bound plane, wishing he were doing no such thing. But he'd felt it impossible to refuse his father in this after his father's reaction to what he'd told him. He'd expected another explosion of rage—but it had been just the opposite.

He still could not credit it.

He'd also felt, because of that completely unexpected reaction from his father to what he'd had to tell him, that he was in no position to refuse his request.

'My boy, I understand completely! But, look, now that you have told me—and I am so very glad you have!—will you agree to what I say now? When you disappeared off grid as you did, the New York deal was so very nearly agreed—it is a pity to abandon it after all your preliminary work on it. So will you not go there now, get it over the line, and come back in a couple of days?' He'd clapped him genially on the back. 'What do you say?'

Nikos had said yes, though it was the last thing he'd wanted to do. But, given how supportive and understanding his father was being—not at all what he'd been anticipating—how could he have refused? As his father had said, he'd be back in a couple of days. And then—

But he would not allow himself to run on ahead. He would get this damn New York trip out of the way first.

He sat back, seat belt fastened, willing the plane to take off. The sooner he was in New York, the sooner he'd be back...

Alys followed Spiros across the atrium, flip-flops flapping noisily on the marble floor, her alarm increasing. Spiros had opened the door of a room on the far side that she had never been into.

'Please wait here,' he told her.

It was some kind of office, filled with high-tech kit, its window obscured by Venetian blinds. She heard footsteps sounding in the hall, and a voice—not Nikos's—addressing Spiros in Greek in stentorian tones. Then someone was walking into the office, shutting the door behind him with a snap.

Alys did a double take. The man was a middle-aged version of Nikos—but not quite. He was not as tall, and nowhere near as jaw-droppingly handsome, even allowing for the difference in age, and he was starting to run to fat, with greying hair and an ill-tempered look about him.

His eyes—like gimlets and starting to pouch—went to the visible evidence of her advancing pregnancy. She saw his expression harden. Then his gaze came back to her face, and she saw something twist in it.

'I am Nikos's father,' announced the man who looked so like Nikos—but not in a good way. 'And he has sent me here to sort out this mess once and for all.' He looked at her, and his expression was pitiless. 'It is all arranged. You are to return to Athens now.' Scorn bit in the dark eyes. 'The time has come for proof. No more prevarication! He has told me he needs to know—is the baby you are flaunting his?'

The blood drained from Alys's face, shock jagging through her as if she had just been punched. She heard the words he was barking out at her now.

'There will be a paternity test! Now—before you give birth. This time you will not refuse.'

She felt herself reel, clutch at the corner of the desk for support, because the room seemed to be swirling around her, and her legs were starting to buckle.

'No…' The word scraped past Alys's throat, hoarse and harsh. 'No! I will not have any such test—I will not! Nikos never said… He would never… Not now…not when…'

Shock was making her incoherent. More than shock—a desperate rejection of what was being said to her. Everything she'd thought real was crashing down around her.

Not Nikos! No, not him—not wanting this!

He'd accepted that the baby was theirs—of course he had! How could it possibly be otherwise?

He cannot think that of me—not now! Not after all we have been to each other here.

She stared, her face white, still disbelieving what was impossible to believe.

Derision was etched across Nikos's father's face. 'Did you think he would not insist? My son is not the fool you take him for!'

'Where is he?' Alys cried, as the air was crushed from her lungs, blood drumming in her ears. 'Where is Nikos?'

She couldn't bear this—it was dreadful, hideous. She would not believe it…could not…

'On his way to New York,' came the harsh answer. 'On my advice. I told him I would deal with you. The maids are packing your things—go and make yourself decent! We leave for Athens immediately!'

Alys's eyes distended and her grip on the corner of the desk tightened. It was all that was keeping her upright.

'I won't go,' she said.

Shock, dismay, horror…all were swallowing her up.

'There can be only one reason for your refusal.' Nikos's father's voice was harsh, his eyes boring into hers like drills. 'And it shows him what he has feared from the start—that you know the baby in your belly is not his! So, do you still refuse to take the test that he demands? Answer me!'

The blood was pounding in her chest, and she felt as if there was a garotte around her throat, but she managed to speak. To say all that was left for her to say.

'Yes…' she said faintly. 'I refuse.'

'Then you will be driven to the airport and a direct flight to England will be arranged—today. You will make no further attempt to contact my son. He has no further interest in you.' Nikos's father's voice twisted again—viciously. 'He will not have another man's bastard to raise.'

Alys heard no more. Could not bear to.

She turned and stumbled from the room.

CHAPTER THIRTEEN

NIKOS LET HIMSELF into his hotel room in Manhattan, a wave of jet lag and tiredness hitting him like a wall. On deplaning, after a flight spent going through the complex and intricate details of the proposal and planning his negotiating strategy, he'd gone straight into a dinner meeting with the other parties, which had been long and intensive.

More meetings were scheduled for the morning, but with luck he might hammer out a mutually acceptable agreement and be back at JFK for the flight home by the evening.

His face shadowed. Would it really be as simple as his father had promised?

He fished his phone out of his jacket pocket. Still no messages or voicemail. He frowned, disquieted. Suppressing an impulse to call, he reminded himself it was hardly dawn in Greece yet.

Another wave of jet lag and tiredness hit him. He would get some shut-eye first, then phone as soon as he awoke.

But when he did, and heard what the voice on the

other end of the phone was telling him, all thought
of the morning's meetings vanished. Within half
an hour he was in the hotel's limo, heading back
to JFK.

Driven by demons.

Alys let herself into her house, exhaustion—more
than exhaustion—filling her. The journey back to
the UK had been gruelling.

Andreas had driven her to the island's airport,
where she'd had to wait for a flight. The only one
direct to the UK had been to Manchester, leaving in the evening. She'd landed after midnight,
and then waited at the airport for the first coach
south to Birmingham. Then she'd got the bus to
her home town and walked from the bus station.

Now she felt like a zombie, hardly able to put
one foot in front of another.

She closed the front door behind her, treading on
a heap of accumulated mail. Wearily she scooped
it up, dumped it on the kitchen table. The house
smelt stale and airless. She had not expected to be
away so long. Nor to come back like this.

Destroyed.

What other word could there be? All her stupid,
pathetic hopes had been ripped from her. Trampled
into the ground.

Tears sprang into her eyes, burning like acid.
She had not allowed herself to cry since fleeing the
villa, knowing that if she started she would never

stop. Even now she blinked them away, lugging her suitcase upstairs, then turning the immersion heater on so she could shower in a while, before going back downstairs to put the kettle on.

She sorted through the mail. Most was junk, but the one she wanted to see was there, and she tore it open, needing to see it in black and white.

Confirmation of the removal of any threat to instigate foreclosure proceedings and the information that her mortgage account was now three months in credit.

She shut her eyes, squeezing acid tears.

At least I saved my home.

Even if she dared not stay in it.

Cold snaked through her veins and her eyes flared open, going out over the small rear garden, its lawn overgrown, pot plants wilting. Another image overlayed it, vivid with bougainvillea, drenched in hot sunshine, girdled by the azure Aegean.

Then it was gone.

Anguish, raw and agonising, crushed her like a vice.

Gone for ever now.

She gave a choke, a cry that was the sound of her heart breaking.

And then the tears came…

Nikos was at his father's house again, striding in, handing his suitcase and his briefcase to the manservant, startled at his unexpected arrival.

'Where is my father?' Nikos's demand was grim. As grim as the expression in his face.

'Kyrios Drakis is at breakfast,' the manservant informed him.

Nikos strode past him, throwing open the doors to the palatial dining room. His father looked up from his place at the head of the table.

'Nikos?' he exclaimed. 'Why are you back so soon? You gave me no indication that—'

Nikos cut across him, slamming shut the doors behind him. This was not for the ears of staff or servants. Only for his father.

His eyes blazed with a cold, deadly light.

'What the *hell*,' he said, 'have you done?'

Alys was packing her suitcase. Not the small carry-on she'd taken to Greece, but a hefty one that would hold enough to see her through into winter. Her expression was set and she worked methodically, her mind racing through the things she still had to do before she could shut the front door and head to the coach station.

A set of house keys was already with the estate agent she'd signed up to put the house on the market. She would let them have a forwarding address once she was settled.

As to where that would be—that was the least of her worries. The only imperative was that it must be far enough away for Nikos never to find her...

Anguish stabbed her, as it had been doing ever

since she'd fled his father, and tears were trying to sting her eyes. She blinked them away. There was no time for tears until she was safely out of the house—safely on a coach to anywhere she could think of.

Nikos's father sat back in his chair.

'What have I *done*?' he echoed. He lifted his hands. 'I have saved you—that's what I've done! Just as I did when Miriam Kapoulou so nearly trapped you. When you were so besotted with her, wet behind the ears! Well, I've done it again— saved you from another of her kind!' His face darkened. 'This time by using the exact same tactics that trapped *me*! I *vowed*, my son, that I would never let it happen to you! And now it won't.' There was triumph in his eyes. 'I've sent her packing— you are free of her!'

Nikos's expression was frozen. 'Free…?' There was a hollow ring to his voice.

'Yes, *free*!' his father repeated. 'She's gone back to England, tail between her legs—I told her that if she refused a paternity test it would be proof that she knew all along her brat was not yours! And she did refuse. Refused outright! So clearly you are *not* the father—and your fate will *not* be mine!'

An oath broke from Nikos. 'Of *course* I am the father!' His voice was twisted, bitterness ripping through it. 'And the fate you have tried to save me from is the only one I long for!' He looked at his father, face stark. 'She is the woman I love,' he said. 'And you have driven her away.'

There was desolation in his voice.

Alys peered out of the sitting room window over the wintry Yorkshire moorland. The holiday rental cottage was going cheap for the off season, but come the spring she would move out into the small but inexpensive flat she was buying in nearby Sheffield, now that the sale of her house had finally gone through.

By then she would be mother to the child who was now within a fortnight of being born. A child who would be as fatherless as she had been.

Better that than a man like Nikos for a father.

Familiar anguish filled her, as it had ever since her return to England, with her stupid, pathetic hopes and dreams in tatters. Her heart in pieces.

But what use was anguish or heartbreak? Only her baby mattered now, and she was all prepared for its arrival. Her hospital bag was packed and her little car—not much more than an old banger, which she'd bought locally—was parked outside the cottage. She'd already stopped working at the travel agency, which had taken her on during the busy high season in summer, after she'd fled her home, terrified that Nikos might come after her.

He must never find me! I could not bear it!

She gazed blindly out of the cottage window, memories crowding, each one an agony.

The hot sun bright on the blue sea...the pool sparkling in the sunshine...the brilliant crimson of the bougainvillea tumbling over the pristine white of the villa's walls...

And most agonising of all...

Nikos—oh, Nikos! Holding out his arms to me, taking my hand, laughing with me, kissing me, making love to me...

She tore her mind away, and it was as painful as if she were tearing her own flesh, turning away from the window.

Outside, unnoticed by her, caught as she was in her own inconsolable grief for what could never be, the first few flakes of snow drifted down out of the leaden sky. Then whirled down faster.

The SUV made its slow way along a lane that was narrowing between drystone walls as it climbed up to the open moor. The light was fading fast and snow was falling—light at first, then more heavily, whirled by the wind across the exposed landscape, thickening to become a blizzard.

His face increasingly grim, its driver pressed on relentlessly...nearing his destination.

Alys drew the thick curtains, then put more wood on the log burner. It was not comfortable to think that she was alone here in this isolated cottage in weather like this. But all she had to do, she told herself sternly, was hunker down and stay indoors.

She had food, she had warmth, she had hot water and she would be fine—just fine.

She settled down on the sofa, flicking through TV channels idly. She came across a programme about moving to warmer climes, finding a holiday home in the Med…whitewashed houses and crimson bougainvillea and azure sea…

Just like her memories.

She changed channel abruptly. No point remembering. It was gone. And so was Nikos.

For ever.

She found an old film, reached for her mug of tea.

A noisy car chase on screen blanked out the sound of a car engine in the real world. But it was not sufficient, a few moments later, to blank out the sudden hard and heavy rapping on the front door of the cottage.

Who on earth…?

She got up, walking to the door in her ungainly fashion, unbolting it and hefting it open to admit a blast of icy wind.

And Nikos.

He strode in, snow whitening his hair and shoulders after just walking the short distance from the SUV pulled up outside the tiny front garden.

Alys had reared back, and his eyes went to her immediately, shock knifing through him. He had known her pregnancy would be advanced by now, but to see her so physically altered from what he remembered was a shock.

Shock was in her eyes too.

And disbelief.

And absolute rejection.

With the flat of his hand he shut the heavy front door, cutting out the freezing wind and snow, stepping towards her. She jerked away, clutching the frame of the door into the sitting room he could see beyond.

'Get out of here!' Her face was contorting. 'Go away! Leave me alone!'

He tried to speak.

'Alys, I—'

'Get out!' Her voice was a shriek now, high-pitched and frantic. Her face was as white as a sheet.

And then a cry broke from her. The look on her face was aghast. She froze, features distended, completely paralysed.

Alarm knifed in him. 'What—?'

She stared at him, that same dreadful, horrified expression on her face. Her eyes were round with disbelief. With terror.

'My waters have broken,' she said, in a voice that was completely blank.

He carried her out to the SUV. It was already almost invisible in the white-out, but he yanked open the passenger door, managing to place the towels he'd grabbed at her stricken direction on the seat. He slammed the door shut, before going back into the cottage to check that the wood burner was safely closed, to collect the hospital bag from her bedroom and lock the front door.

He got back into the SUV.

She was leaning back in her seat, eyes closed. For a second a memory stabbed of how he'd driven her, after her excoriating meltdown, from the island airport to the villa, and she had kept her eyes closed for the entire journey, shutting him out.

She was shutting him out again.

Emotion stabbed at him like a piercing dagger. But he had no time for that—not now. Now there was only one priority.

'Get the hospital on the phone…warn them we're on our way,' he told her.

He put the SUV into four-wheel drive—essential in these appalling conditions—and inched his way forward, hoping the snow drifts forming already would not be too high.

The journey down to the town in the dale below was a nightmare. He was barely able to see through the blizzard. He passed abandoned vehicles, a snow plough heading elsewhere, conscious all the time of Alys, face white, eyes closed.

And then her face contorted, her hands pressing over her distended abdomen, eyes flying open.

'Oh, God, that was a contraction! *Nikos*—'

Her voice was high-pitched. Terrified.

He reached for her hand. 'It will be OK,' he said. 'It will be OK. I'll get you there in time.'

He drove on, face set and grimmer still.

By the time he pulled up at the hospital her contractions were quickening. He leapt from the car, ran into the entrance lobby, yelling he knew not what. Then other people were running. Paramedics were coming out to the parked car, still with its hazard lights flashing, getting Alys out, lowering her onto a trolley, racing away with her.

He wanted to follow, but could not leave the SUV there, blocking the way. He went to park it, then ran back as fast as the driving snow would let him. Inside, he saw the signs to Maternity and vaulted up the stairs, nor bothering to wait for the lift. There was a reception desk at the entrance, and urgently he asked where Alys had been taken.

They would not tell him.

'She told us not to admit you,' the receptionist said. 'To ask you to leave.'

He made no answer, just numbly went to the waiting area and sat down on a hard chair, his heart pounding, staring at nothing.

He would not leave. He would wait here.

For ever, if he had to.

Nothing else was possible for him.

CHAPTER FOURTEEN

ALYS WAS SITTING up in the hospital bed, the morning sunlight frail after the night's snowstorm. She was as weak as a kitten, her body aching, but what was that to her? Beside her, in a little crib, her baby slept.

Emotion poured through her, overwhelming her. Gratitude, profound and abject, filled her, because her baby was safe and well.

A knock came at the door, and a nurse put her head around it. 'You have a visitor!' she said brightly.

She didn't stop to check whether Alys wanted a visitor or not.

Nikos walked in.

Her face stiffened instantly. 'I don't want you here!'

She saw him pause by the door, shut it quietly, but firmly.

'And I don't want to *be* here either!' Alys forged on. 'You had no right to have me transferred to the private wing, to a room of my own! I would have been fine on the maternity ward!'

He ignored her protest, instead taking a chair and drawing it forward a little, sitting himself down upon it.

Her eyes went to him, baleful.

Defensive.

Because there was so much she had to defend herself from. From the past, and the present—and the future.

And she must defend herself, too, from something she was helpless to defend herself against.

He sat there, leaning forward slightly, his hands resting, upturned, on his strong thighs, his muscled torso moulded by a dark slate cashmere sweater, his eyes boring into her, darker yet.

Every centimetre of him was familiar to her—once precious to her.

But never again—dear God, never again!

She felt tears, hot and utterly unnecessary, prick behind her eyelids, but she would not admit to them. Would not admit to the buckling emotion convulsing through her, the longing filling her.

A longing that could never be slaked.

A love she could never have.

Not now. Not ever.

It mocked her with the poisoned tips of a whip that bit into her flesh, flailing her for her own blindness, her own stupidity, her own unforgivable folly in coming to trust him as she had, falling in love with him…

And all along—dear God—it was a ploy, a pretence, a charade on his part! Every word he spoke to me, every smile, every kiss and caress, a lie.

The pain lashed across her again—pain she must endure for the rest of her life…

But she would not let it show. She would *not*. She would never, *never* let him see how he had hurt her. Destroyed her…

'Alys…' his voice was low, and she had to strain to hear him '…we have to talk.'

She shook her head. 'No, we don't,' she answered him. 'And if you want me to thank you for getting me here in time—well, if you hadn't turned up like that I wouldn't have gone into labour because of the shock!'

A grave expression passed across his face. 'Do you think I don't know that?' he said heavily.

She saw his eyes slip from her down to the crib on the far side of the bed. There was a hungry look in his face. She wondered at it, then hardened her heart.

'It's not yours,' she told him. Her voice was flat. 'I fell into bed with another man the day after I slept with you. So you can keep your precious Drakis money, and not waste a penny of it raising another man's bastard!'

His face whitened, lines knifing around his

mouth. 'Don't speak like that—' The words broke from him.

She snaked forward, her voice a vicious hiss, eyes venomous. 'Why not? It's what you said to me in Athens! And it's what your father said to me at the villa! When you sent him to do your dirty work for you!'

Nikos's eyes blazed with black fire at her accusation. 'I did not send him!' he ground out. 'Disbelieve anything you will about me, but believe this—I *did not* send him!'

She saw him shut his eyes, clench his hands. Then slowly, forcibly, he opened his hands, his eyes.

He was looking right at her.

'I have something I must tell you,' he said.

Tension was racking through Nikos as he started to speak, to say what he must. His voice was halting, but he made himself go on.

'When we ate at that taverna in the harbour, you asked about my mother. I didn't want to talk about her. I never have. She left for California when I was barely two years old—I have no memories of her and do not want any.' His voice changed, hardened. 'My father had quite enough of them to pass on to me. And I've heard them all my life.' His mouth pressed tightly. 'An endless litany that never stops.'

His gaze slid away. Away from the crib he could not see into on the far side of her bed. Away out of the window, looking over the hospital's busy car park. Away into the past. A past that was not his, but a past that had shaped him, warped him.

'My father met my mother when she was working as a hostess in a club on one of Greece's party islands—the kind of place my father liked to hang out at when he was young…not just for the party atmosphere, free and easy after the strictures of his own upbringing, but because of women like my mother. Women who liked men with lots of money to spend on them, squander on them, before they moved on to someone else. But my mother didn't intend my father to move on to another woman. So she deliberately got herself pregnant. Yes—' he held up a hand '—I know. It takes two. But she lied to him about contraception, and he was…caught.'

His eyes came back to Alys. Her face was expressionless, but he could see something in the depths of her eyes that made him go on.

'Caught,' he said again, quite deliberately. And then he went on, incising each word, 'And he has continued, for his entire life, to think of himself that way.' And now he could not stop another note entering his voice—one that seemed to come from so deep down that it drew blood…his blood. 'Left to himself he would never have troubled to marry her just because she was pregnant—a nightclub hostess, marrying a Drakis! Unthinkable! But his own father was strait-laced. He insisted on the marriage, refused to tolerate any scandal, any Drakis bastards—' he had to force himself to say the word

'—that might taint the family's pristine reputation. My father caved in—furious and reluctant, but not wanting to endanger his own inheritance.'

He looked away again, out through the window.

'All his life he has loathed my mother with a fury that time has not dimmed. Claiming she ruined his life, saddled him with me—' He broke off, still not looking back at Alys. 'And even though all the tests he insisted on proved I was his, I was still never the son he wanted... How could I be, with a mother like mine?'

He drew a breath, whipping his eyes back to Alys. She was sitting there very still, motionless. Eyes veiled.

'I've had to prove every single day of my life that I am a Drakis.' Each word was ground out like glass. 'Doing what a Drakis does—'

'Making money.' Alys's words fell into the gaping space between them. 'Keeping it safe from women like your mother. From women like me.'

He couldn't read her voice—there was no expression in it. He only nodded, his eyes slipping away again. Towards the crib he still could not see into.

'When I read your letter telling me you were pregnant,' he said, 'I—'

'Saw history repeating itself.' Alys cut across him. 'I get the picture, Nikos.' Her voice was tight—so tight it could have strangled him.

He fought for a breath, which razored in his

throat when he saw the way she was looking at him. 'Not quite,' he said in a low voice.

He swallowed, and it was as if a stone was lodged there and he could not breathe past it. A stone that had lodged there a long, long time ago.

'You see, Alys, I do not see the world through the eyes of a man trapped into fathering a child he did not want by a woman he did not want. I see the world through the eyes of an unwanted child.' His eyes came back to her, open and unflinching. 'The unwanted child I was.' His fingers clenched again. 'Which is why, Alys, neither you nor I could ever be important in this. Only one human being is important.'

He would not let his gaze go to the crib— would *not*.

'Any child…*every* child…deserves parents who want them and are deserving of them. Deserves as decent a childhood as possible. In Athens, I wanted us to marry because I did not want any stigma— any taint, any doubt at all—to haunt the child you carried.' He swallowed, and still that stone blocking his throat would not shift. 'And I wanted an *in utero* DNA test because if we'd married first and had the test done after you gave birth, and it had showed…well, that the father was another man, it would have been a mess all round. You would have had no chance to contact the other man, maybe marry him, ensure the baby was legitimate—'

He stood up suddenly, striding to the window,

whipping round to look at her. He must say what he had to say—the only important thing to say.

'It was the baby I had to protect, Alys—not me!'

She was looking at him, and he could not bear the way she was doing it.

'You could have told me that,' she said.

There was no emotion in her voice. It was completely empty, like her eyes, which were looking at him in the way he could not bear. But must.

'I couldn't take the risk,' he answered. 'It would have shown you I had a weak point…that I cared about the baby you carried. You could have used it as a weapon against me, as my mother used me to get a ring on her finger, and an eye-watering divorce settlement that has made her a rich woman. It's what made me so…so harsh towards you in Athens. I wanted you to be intimidated by me… cowed.'

He took another razoring breath.

'But it backfired on me. Sent you fleeing, and into that meltdown at the airport. I realised then…' and now his gaze at her was naked '…that I needed to change tactics.'

'By taking me to the villa.' Alys's fingers twisted in the coverlet. Her eyes dropped. 'Taking me to bed. Neutralising me.'

Her words dropped like stones.

'Yes.' The admission fell from him. As necessary now as his impulsive decision to take her to Villa Drakis had been necessary then. 'I had to stop you resisting me. I had to make you compliant.' A nerve was ticking in his cheek, but he could not stop it. 'I had to make you willing to stay with me while I—'

'Softened me up so I'd be willing to have that DNA test.'

Again, Alys's words cut across his. And still there was no expression in her eyes, just her unblinking gaze that was impossible to meet. And yet he must.

And he must say what he said next.

'No.'

A single word, but it seemed to fill the room. Something moved in the depths of her eyes, but he did not know what it was. Knew only that he had to keep speaking.

'It was to give me time to make my mind up about you.'

He saw her fingers clench, entwined in the bedclothes, knuckles whitening.

Restlessly, he moved about the room, then turned.

'And I did,' he said. This time it was his voice, his eyes, that had no expression in them. 'Which is why...' he took a breath that could pass only with difficulty past that stone still lodged in his throat '...why I returned to Athens. There were things I needed to do. Including,' he said, 'talk to my father.'

'Oh, yes,' said Alys. 'Your father. Who wasted

no time before rushing to the villa and sending me packing!'

Bitterness was in her voice now, open and scathing. It scored on Nikos's skin like acid.

'I did *not* send him!' he said again. 'I told him about the situation because I knew I could put it off no longer. I expected him to be furious…' He frowned. 'But he was amazingly forbearing.' His mouth tightened. 'You see, it was not just that he was thinking of his own disastrous marriage.' He took another heavy breath. 'He was thinking of the one I almost made myself.'

He shut his eyes for a moment, in that second seeing the past as vividly as if it had become the present, then opened them again.

'When I was twenty-two I fell for the daughter of one of his business acquaintances. I was besotted with her. She played me along, declaring she loved me—only me! Then my father disclosed to me that her father was close to bankruptcy and a Drakis son-in-law would be a lifeline for his family.' His voice hardened unconsciously. 'He told me that if I insisted on marrying her he would cast me out of the family, disinherit me, leave me penniless. Unlike my father, who buckled under *his* father's threat to disinherit him, I didn't care! I rushed to Miriam, certain she loved me as much as I loved her, certain she wouldn't care that I wouldn't be rich any longer.'

He frowned, as if speaking had become difficult.

'She walked out on me. The very next month married a man who was as old as her father but stinking rich. My father told me he'd taught me an invaluable lesson—told me that never again would I let myself fall in love with a woman who loved the Drakis riches more than me.'

He turned away. Walked back to the window to stare out of it sightlessly.

'So when I told him about you he rode to the rescue again. To save me from his own fate and from the fate that had so nearly engulfed me when I was still wet behind the ears. He was triumphant about it—about what he'd achieved while I'd been despatched off to New York on the pretext of finishing off a half-completed deal out there. Triumphant that he'd sent you packing, saved me from the clutches of yet another gold-digger after the Drakis money.'

He lifted his hand to fiddle with the blind cord, needing something to preoccupy him. Something to stop him thinking about what he would say next.

'But his triumph fell flat.' His voice was expressionless. 'I did not wish to be saved.'

Alys heard him and yet did not hear him. Her heart was thumping in her chest, and maybe it was that that made his words blur in her ears.

Nikos was turning around again, looking at

her again. That familiar veiling was in his eyes, making them quite impossible to read. To dare to read...

'Since the moment I read your letter, telling me you were pregnant, I have had to face the fact that not only might the baby not be mine, but that you might be cut from the same cloth as my mother. Wanting only my money.'

Two spots of colour burned in Alys's cheeks.

'I did, Nikos. I did want your money.' She would not flinch from meeting his eyes. 'To pay off my debts, like I told you.'

'Why did you have debts, Alys? I tried to find out at the villa, but you would not tell me. So tell me now.'

His eyes were levelled at her. She gave a shrug. No point being evasive now. 'The mortgage on my house was in arrears. They were threatening foreclosure. I couldn't risk it—not with a baby on its way.'

'Why in arrears, Alys?'

His voice was persistent, his gaze still levelled at her. She swallowed. 'My mother was the victim of a hit-and-run accident that left her very badly injured. She couldn't work any longer, and I had to leave uni to be her carer. Money was incredibly tight, and that's how the arrears crept up. When she died last year the mortgage company wanted full repayment or they would issue proceedings for repossession. That's why I took your money, Nikos—'

She broke off, incapable of more. Emotion was heaving in her—unbearable, impossible. But she must not let it.

Her fingers twisted in the bedclothes again, whitening her knuckles. 'Look, just *go*, Nikos! I don't want you, I don't need you, and I don't need your money! I've sold my house, and there was enough equity to let me buy a one-bedroom flat. So I'll be fine, Nikos—just fine! I don't need any more of your money! So you can go and tell your precious father that he did, indeed, save you from a woman like your mother.'

She slumped back against the pillows, exhausted in body, and in mind, and in her stupid, battered broken heart.

'But my father didn't save me, Alys. He destroyed me.'

Nikos's voice was weary, drained of all emotion. Emotion that had had to be drained out of him, painfully and completely, in the months since his father had told him what he'd done.

Emotion he had no right to.

Would never have a right to.

Not any more.

He would tell her why. It might assuage her. Give her some satisfaction, however belated.

'You have every right to be angry with me, Alys.

From the moment you told me about the baby I suspected you, accused you, condemned you and manipulated you—seduced you, lied to you. I treated you shamefully.'

He frowned.

'But these last months have been unendurable. You vanished, Alys. I could not reach you from New York, and when I phoned Spiros he told me my father had been and you had left the island. I confronted my father, and he told me what he'd done. I was desperate! But I could not find you... The estate agent handling the sale of your house would say nothing to me, and in the end I had to hire private investigators, who finally managed to track you down.'

'You shouldn't have bothered, Nikos,' he heard her say.

He flinched. The hostility in her voice was like a knife's stab. 'I had to,' he said. 'I had to find you! Find you and tell you—' He broke off. Was there any use in telling her? Was there any use in being here at all?

Except...

He felt his eyes go towards the far side of the bed, to the crib he could not see into.

'Tell you that I would give everything for my father not to have done what he did,' he said heavily—though to what purpose he did not know, for was she not lost to him for ever now, fleeing from him as she had, hiding from him, rejecting him?

That stab came again, as if the blade was twisting in his guts. 'I would give everything not to have you believe I'm still the same man I was when you first came to Athens.'

Something moved in his face now, in his voice.

'Because I am not that man any longer! On the island, at the villa—yes, I wanted to make you mine, to win you over. Because I did not want you fleeing back to England again, taking our baby with you! A baby I *knew* was mine, for how else would I so desire you? But in those weeks I spent with you, Alys, I came to realise it was not just because of the baby—it was because of *you*. You, Alys. And I wanted you so, so much—just as I told you. Wanted more and more for there to be the *us* I told you I wanted! Those weeks I had with you at the villa…' He took a razored breath. 'They were the happiest of my life—'

He paused, gazing down at her. She had no expression on her face—none at all. But he knew he must keep speaking. He had sought her for months, and now had found her—he would say all that was within him. And then he would leave. Because she did not want him—would never want him.

He felt that knife twist in his guts again, pain convulsing him.

'That is why I knew I had to go to Athens,' he said. 'Knew I had to confront my father, and tell him…' he took another razored breath '…that I had fallen in love with you.' His face worked. 'I hoped he would accept it and welcome you as my beloved wife. Instead he destroyed all my hopes by driving you away as he did.'

He turned away, walking to the door—for there was no point staying any longer. No point at all.

Hand on the doorknob, he turned. 'I will leave you now, as you wish me to do. I will make arrangements for sufficient funds to be available for you so that you lack nothing as you raise your baby.' His voice thickened. 'The baby I make no claim to.'

For the last time he let his eyes go to the far side of her bed, to the crib he could not see into. There was a hunger inside him that could never be assuaged now. For his baby…for the woman he loved…

Her voice stayed him.

'I think you mean, Nikos, *our* baby.'

Alys saw him freeze, then slowly, very slowly, turn around. But it was hard to see him clearly. Silent tears were running down her cheeks and her vision was blurred with them.

'Come and see,' she said to him.

She watched him come haltingly, through her blurred vison, and go round to the crib side of the bed.

As if on cue, the tiny baby within stirred, securely wrapped and covered, one tiny starfish hand uncurling. Giving a tiny yawn, it opened its eyes. Gazing at Nikos with pale blue incomprehension.

'Say hello to our daughter, Nikos,' Alys said, and her voice was a whisper, because anything else was impossible.

'She's perfect… Our perfect, perfect baby.'

It was Nikos speaking, his voice husky, but it could have been her—for, as it happened, that was exactly her opinion of their baby too.

Our baby.

The simple pronoun convulsed within her.

A sob broke from her. 'Oh, Nikos, she is *ours*, isn't she?' It was an imprecation, a plea.

Her hand was seized. Crushed.

'For ever!'

Her other hand was seized, and then Nikos was sinking down on the bed, his eyes pouring into hers.

'Do you mean it? Do you truly mean it, Alys? *Can* you mean it, after the way I've treated you? I would give all the world to undo that!'

She let her hands be crushed in his, because their strength was hers now—all hers. Wonder filled her, and a joy so fierce she could barely bear it. But she knew it was a joy that she would bear all her life now.

'I fell in love with you at the villa, Nikos! And all I wanted, with all my heart, was to make a family with you—you and me and our baby.'

Her face convulsed.

'It hurt me so *much*, Nikos, when your father came! Ripping my hopes from me! Hating me so much—'

Tears were pouring down her face, and Nikos was bending forward to kiss them away.

'Don't weep, my dearest, sweetest love—don't weep! I cannot bear it if you weep!'

She only sobbed more, and then his hands were releasing hers and he was wrapping her in his arms, holding her close, so very close. As close as their hearts beat against each other.

Then, as her weeping ceased, she became dimly aware of another sound. A faint, displeased mewing. She drew back, her arms dropping from Nikos, twisting as she sat up to look down into the crib beside the bed.

In her cosy spot in the crib, their daughter's little face was screwed up, her mouth opening, and for a tiny human being her lungs were mighty! Her demand was peremptory and insistent.

Alys carefully scooped her up, peeling back her gown to expose her breast, already tingling on cue, carefully latching her on.

Nikos sat back, giving them space. But he lifted a hand, stretching out one tentative finger to stroke, with infinite gentleness, the cheek of his newborn daughter.

Then his eyes went to Alys. 'Is this really true?' he asked wonderingly. 'That we can go from hell to heaven like this?'

With her free hand she took hold of his, meshing her fingers with his. The joy that had burned with a furnace of fierceness was now the warm, cherishing glow of devotion.

'Wherever the three of us are, it will always be heaven for us, Nikos.'

Her eyes poured into his with all that she felt, all that she saw reflected in his own. And at her breast, their tiny daughter feasted, as much in a state of bliss as her parents, who were now leaning gently forward to kiss again and seal their love for ever.

EPILOGUE

'My dear, may I really not pour some champagne for you? Just a little?'

The voice so like his own was as he had never heard it before, Nikos thought. Kindly, conciliatory—fatherly.

But this was a father such as he had never known before. Wonder filled him, and astonishment too—and above all gratitude.

He watched now as his father, still trying to tempt Alys to replace her innocuous elderflower spritzer with something alcoholic—vintage champagne from his own cellars in the opulent Drakis mansion in Kifissia, inside which they were all gathered—fussed over the woman he had once tried to separate from his son.

Nikos's expression changed. He knew full well what had wrought this extraordinary transformation. His gaze went to the woman he loved beyond life itself and to the baby she held on her lap, regally arrayed in a christening robe of such sumptuousness that Nikos could only profoundly hope that Alys had a muslin to hand in case of untoward posseting.

Love filled his eyes. Love—endless and eternal!—for Alys, who filled his heart and very being, and love—so fiercely, burningly protective and devoted—for the daughter they shared together.

The daughter who was a precious and most beloved granddaughter as well.

Again Nikos felt that wash of wonder and gratitude go through him. He suppressed a wry, private smile as he sipped his own champagne. In those desolate months when he'd been so desperately trying to find Alys, after she'd fled Greece, his father had finally come to realise just how much she meant to his son. And when Nikos had disclosed to his father Alys's devotion to her stricken mother, and the reason she had accumulated the debts she had, it had been all the confirmation his father had needed to know that Alys was nothing like the woman who had trapped him into marriage all those bitter years ago.

That and setting eyes on his granddaughter!

For when Nikos had brought Alys back to Greece, it had been to a reception warmer than he had dared hope for. His father had opened his arms to Alys, his apologies for what he had done so profuse and heartfelt that both Alys and Nikos had had finally to silence him.

They had been married in Yorkshire, as soon as it could be arranged, cosying down, while the necessary paperwork was completed, in the snug little cottage which they had decided to buy as their UK hideaway. Alys had donated her flat in Sheffield for the use of a charity that housed women fleeing domestic abuse.

But preventing his father fussing over and pampering both Alys and their daughter had been impossible—nor did he and Alys try.

'I have not been a good father, my boy—I let my bitterness poison me. Let me now strive to be a good father-in-law. And a good grandfather.'

Nikos felt his throat tighten as he remembered his father's apology. It tightened more as he heard again in his head his father's tentative request that one of their daughter's names be for Nikos's grandmother, who had died while his father was only a teenager himself.

Alys's face had lit up. *'Anatalia? Oh, but that's a beautiful name!'* She'd given a little choke of emotion. *'And my own mother's name was Ann...'*

'Doubly perfect, then!' Nikos had said. *'Our wonderful daughter—named for two wonderful grandmothers!'*

As if she'd heard him thinking her name, their tiny daughter, Anatalia Nikola Alicia—*Ana, indeed*—opened her eyes and gave her little mewing cry, gazing fixedly up at her grandfather.

Nikos's wry smile deepened.

'Aha!' his father announced fondly. 'Now she wakes...our little princess!' He clapped a fatherly hand on Nikos's shoulder. 'We must raise a toast to her, my son, and to my new daughter!' He beamed at both of them.

They all duly raised their glasses as Nikos's father pronounced a traditional Greek blessing on his newly christened granddaughter. Soon, in a matter of weeks, he would be pronouncing another traditional Greek blessing—this time on newly-weds. For Nikos and Alys had conceded to his request that they add to their civil marriage one under Greek Orthodox rites.

All they had insisted on, though, was that they did not want a grand high-society event in Athens, however anxious Nikos's father was to make all the amends he could for his initial opposition to Alys.

So, instead, there was to be a small private wedding in the church in the *agora* in the harbour town on the island, and they would be married from the Villa Drakis, which was to be Nikos and Alys's home.

Nikos would continue to cut down on his work-load, as he already had, minimising his globe-trotting in favour of spending time with Alys and Ana, devoting more time to developing the island's economy—starting with investing in Spiros's cous-in's winery, a bottle from which was already await-ing consumption over dinner, once Ana was abed for the night.

He heard his father give a sigh of pleasure and

satisfaction. 'I am the happiest of men,' he said happily.

Nikos shook his head. 'That cannot be,' he contradicted smilingly. 'For *I* am the happiest of men!'

Alys looked up from discreetly latching Ana on beneath the muslin. 'And *we*,' she informed them, speaking on busy Ana's behalf, 'are the happiest of *women*.'

Her smile embraced them both—her beloved husband, and her doting father-in-law, who was lavishing upon her the fatherly affection she had never known.

Her smile deepened as her eyes focussed on Nikos, meeting his. And in them, as there always would be, was a blaze of radiant joy and love, whose warmth would be an unquenchable fire in his heart all his days, and all his nights, and for all eternity itself.

* * * * *

Caught up in the magic of
Cinderella's Baby Confession?
Then you're sure to love these other
Julia James stories!

Billionaire's Mediterranean Proposal
Irresistible Bargain with the Greek
The Greek's Duty-Bound Royal Bride
The Greek's Penniless Cinderella
Cinderella in the Boss's Palazzo

Available now!